The Princess Who Sang Like a Frog

and Other Tales of Love

CALLIE CARDAMON

Sublimatio Books
Pasadena, CA

First printing, 2021.
ISBN – 13 (hardcover): 9780578965482
ISBN – 13 (epub): 9780578965499

Interior and cover design by *the*BookDesigners
www.bookdesigners.com

The following is a work of fiction created by the author. All names,
individuals, characters, places, items, events, etc. are either the
product of the author or are used fictitiously. Any name, place,
event, person, or item, current or past, is entirely coincidental.

www.calliecardamon.com

This book is dedicated to my parents,
Ernest and Marie Cardamone,
who gave me many magical gifts
to help me on my way.

Contents

1

The Princess Who Sang Like a Frog

151

The Yellow Bird

169

The Woodcutter's Daughter

193

The Joyfish

211

Acknowledgements

One

nce upon a time, when wishing still mattered, a princess lived in a land neither here nor there. Her eyes sparkled like sun on the water, a smile played upon her lips, and her hair flowed in waves all the way to her feet. She was the youngest of the king's thirteen daughters.

In that land, from time immemorial, all princesses had extraordinary singing voices which emerged in their throats on the day they turned sixteen. Each voice was unique, each incredibly beautiful. One voice glistened like morning dew, another bloomed like a scarlet poppy, still another pattered like a rainy afternoon, and one rang as deep as midnight in a secret garden. On the day her voice emerged, each princess sang in public for the first time to share her gift, and suitors came from far and wide to hear her song and to extend offers of marriage.

The first twelve princesses had made their debuts and had charmed all who were lucky enough to hear them. Each had been chosen by a noble prince whose love she had awakened by the power and beauty of her singing.

And so, on the day she turned sixteen, the thirteenth princess stood before her suitors, who were stunned by her tremendous beauty and eager to hear what wondrous voice she would bring forth. The king and queen leaned forward upon their thrones. All the court stood in anticipation. Like her sisters before her, the princess opened her mouth, as curious as the audience to know what extraordinary song she would sing, but alas, she was unable to produce even one note. She blushed, cleared her throat, and tried again. Nothing.

The king and queen gazed at each other in consternation, and the rest of the court stared at their feet in an agony of embarrassment. A princess without a singing voice! Why, that was like a morning without a sun or a night without a moon! The

One

princess was overcome by great shame. Her tender dreams of love and marriage to a noble prince fled from her heart, and she felt herself grow deathly cold. The suitors began to edge away. Obviously, the unlucky maiden was cursed. The king and queen must have offended some powerful fairy or great wizard, and the princess had been punished for their wrongdoing, as often happens.

The palace hall emptied, and she was left standing alone, unchosen.

The royal physician was called at once. He could find nothing wrong with the princess—she was in perfect health—and he was mystified. At last he suggested, rather timidly, that perhaps she had been enchanted. She was, after all, the thirteenth princess, and everyone knew how unfortunate that number could be.

The king sent for the greatest wizards and fairies in the realm for help with the disenchanting. The princess swallowed elixir after elixir, rubbed powdered butterfly wings upon her throat, and slept with daffodils beneath her pillow, but still she was unable to sing a note.

A year passed. Every morning with great faith

and terrible longing, the princess opened her mouth to sing, but to no avail. Her voice remained locked inside of her like a treasure in a chest without a key.

Finally, the king offered half of his kingdom and the princess's hand to the man who could disenchant her, but not one suitor presented himself. The king and queen were heartbroken for their youngest daughter, but they were grateful that she would neither sleep for a hundred years nor be transformed into an animal, as often happens to enchanted princesses. Not being able to sing was sorrowful, but at least she remained awake and human.

But the princess could not accept this strange affliction. She wanted nothing more than to marry a handsome prince whom she had charmed by the power and beauty of her song. She would have been far happier to sleep a hundred years or be turned into a wild animal! At least those enchantments had remedies. After a certain time, an eager prince would ride through the hedge of briar roses and wake the princess, or an unwilling prince would cut off the head and paws of a fox, which would instantly transform into a princess. Difficult, yes, but not impossible, as her case seemed to be.

One

To make matters worse, one terrible day the princess overheard the ladies of the court speculating that perhaps something was wrong with her heart, for it was common knowledge that singing came from the heart. "A princess without a heart is a frightening thing," one of the ladies said, and they all shivered. "Terribly unnatural!" said another. This was more than the princess could bear.

"Could it be that I have no heart?" she asked herself. And she wept to think of her emptiness and wondered why she had been punished so.

That night, after one final, fruitless attempt to sing, the princess realized that she no longer wished to live in a land where she would never be loved but only pitied or feared. She wrapped herself in a cloak and stole away from the castle.

Two

The princess walked for many miles, absorbed by her unhappy thoughts, until she was far from the countryside to which she was accustomed. A bird's sharp cry returned her to awareness, and she found herself in the middle of a lush forest graced with an abundance of intoxicating wildflowers and magnificent trees. Animal songs filled the air with music so exquisite that the princess momentarily forgot her pain. Overcome by weariness and lulled by the strange melodies, she sank to the earth and fell fast asleep.

She awoke beneath a full moon and breathed in the heady fragrance of the forest. The animals were quiet now, but in the distance, she detected a human voice. It was rich and deep, far deeper than any of her sisters' voices. She listened with great interest and a little fear—what sort of woman would sing thus? Mesmerized, she rose and walked as if in a trance toward the enchanting voice. Stepping into a clearing, she spied a young man sitting beside a pond—and singing! The princess had never heard a man sing before. It was quite preposterous! Everyone knew that women sang, and men married them for their singing. In all her life she had never conceived of this possibility—a man who could create his own music. She grew more and more fascinated as she listened, until finally she cried, "Young man! What are you doing?"

"I am singing." He laughed. "Have you never heard a man sing before?"

"No," she whispered shyly. "I have never."

"And have you never sung before, lovely girl?" he asked with a smile.

"Young man," she whispered, "I can neither sing nor love, for there is something wrong with my heart."

"What is wrong with it?" asked he with kind concern.

"I do not know," she said earnestly. "All my sisters before me have been able to sing, as you were singing a moment ago, and their singing drew their husbands to them. I, however, am unable to sing, and it is commonly believed that my heart is at fault. Apparently, I have been enchanted in a most unusual way, and until I am disenchanted, I am unworthy of a man's love and must pass my life in loneliness." Her eyes filled with tears.

"Are you in love then?" the young man asked.

"No," said she, surprised by this question. "That is not how it works in my land. A prince will fall in love with me when he hears me sing."

The young man persisted in his questions. "Will you then fall in love? After he has chosen you?"

The princess was silent. "I do not know," she said finally. "I never thought to wonder nor to ask my older sisters if that is the way it works."

The young man considered her answer. "Could there not be another reason for your problem?" he offered. "What if you are unable to sing because you have not found the proper man to sing to? What if you need to fall in love before you can sing?"

Now this the princess had never considered, nor had anyone in her kingdom, not even the wisest and oldest of the wizards and fairies. She felt a glimmer of hope begin to grow in her heart. She looked at the young man with great gratitude. "Perhaps," she began thoughtfully, "I am not as flawed as I have believed. Perhaps there is nothing wrong with my heart."

"I think that is true," said he. "For I can see your heart shining in the back of your eyes, and it is quite lovely."

The princess blushed deeply and turned away. She wanted desperately to believe him but could not release her doubt. "Young man," she said sadly, "I am grateful for your kind words, but I will only know the truth about my heart the day I hear myself sing, as I heard you singing. That is my greatest wish. And I will not return to my home until I can do so."

"Your country's customs seem odd," he replied, "but if you believe in your path, you must follow it. Good luck to you," he said and then closed his eyes and returned to his song.

Three

The princess continued her journey, following no compass, seeking no path. Her encounter with the singing man seemed dreamlike, and after many miles, the memory of his kind words disappeared. She was once again alone with her unhappy thoughts. She wanted only to find a land where she could be free to live as she was—imperfect and unworthy of love but meaning no harm to anyone.

A bird cried in the distance, and she turned toward its sound. Soon she entered a forest teeming with animal songs—chirping, growling, hissing, croaking—such strange and beautiful music! One song was far louder than the others—and closer. Sensing movement at her feet, the princess glanced down at the largest frog she had ever seen. Surely a king!

"Dear Frog King," she said as she bowed. "I am charmed by your deep and resounding voice. Fortunate are you to be granted such a gift!"

Despite the princess's disheveled appearance after weeks of travel, her graceful manners revealed her royal stature, and the Frog King bowed as well. "Princess, I am honored that you find my singing voice acceptable, for I have been told by many others that it is abysmal." He croaked with pleasure.

"They must not know what a gift it is to produce a song at all," the princess said. And she told him the story of her failure to sing in court and why she had chosen to leave her home.

The Frog King listened thoughtfully. "I have never heard of such a predicament. Surely, all creatures can sing. Perhaps you lack a teacher."

"There are no singing teachers in my land," she replied, "for none have ever been necessary. Besides," she added, "the problem may not rest only with my voice; my heart, too, may be at fault." She stared at him with such a piteous look that the Frog King's eyes filled with tears.

Three

"I cannot believe there is anything wrong with your heart," he said. "You seem to be a kind young woman. Perhaps I can teach you to sing."

"But how?" asked the princess.

"If you would let me kiss you," he said, "I believe I might awaken your singing voice."

This seemed unusual but hardly more unusual than anything else in her life. She knelt before the Frog King, who hopped on her shoulder and pressed his bright green mouth on her throat.

At once the princess felt a strange stirring in her tongue. She opened her mouth, and—lo and behold!—a croaking sound emerged. And although it was not the voice that she had imagined for herself, it was nonetheless miraculous. Her body thrilled as she croaked, her voice growing stronger and stronger.

"Such exquisite singing!" cried the Frog King, joining her in song. Soon hundreds of frogs hopped to her side. They croaked together for hours in a joyous chorus and danced a wild green dance.

Finally, the princess stopped to catch her breath. "I can never thank you enough!" she said, barely able to speak for the happiness that arose in her throat.

"I must return home at once to sing for my suitors!"

"Not yet, Princess," said the Frog King. "With your new voice comes new responsibility."

The princess could barely conceal her disappointment. "Forgive my impatience, but I have waited so long."

"So, too, has another waited," said the Frog King. "Listen carefully. You must practice your new voice with devotion as you go deeper into the forest. Soon you will meet someone who will give you good advice. You will be wise to follow it. And remember this:

Things are not what they may seem;
A nightmare may become a dream.
What seems cold and made of stone
May change its form by love alone.

With these words the Frog King gave a resounding croak, and out of his mouth popped a large emerald shaped like an eye, which he dropped into the princess's hand. She stared with wonder at this gift. "Keep this with you always," he said. "It will protect you and save another's life." With a mighty leap, the Frog King disappeared into the forest.

Three

The princess placed the eye-shaped emerald in a velvet bag she wore around her neck and continued along her way.

Four

Intent upon fulfilling her responsibility so that she could return home, the princess continued her journey. She croaked as she walked, practicing her singing with devotion, and growing more confident in her voice. One day, however, she found herself recalling her dreadful debut. How eagerly she had opened her mouth to sing only to be denied what all other princesses had received! With this humiliating memory, her despair returned. As grateful as she was for her new voice, she began to doubt its beauty. It was quite different from any princess's voice she had ever heard. What if this croaking sound brought her nothing but shame? The thought of a loveless future overwhelmed her.

She sank to the ground and began to weep.

"Greetings, Princess," said a kind voice. "I have been waiting for you."

The princess looked up to see a young man seated beside her. "You have?" she asked. "But who are you? You seem familiar, and yet I cannot place you."

"Are you certain you do not recognize me?" he asked with a smile.

The princess stared into his eyes for a long time. Finally, she said, "I seem to recall meeting a young man like you once, but I cannot for the life of me remember where or when."

"Perhaps this will remind you." He threw back his head, and out flew a song of such majesty and joy that the princess beamed with delight.

"I remember now! I met you many miles ago. The marvelous singing man who spoke kind words. Teach me to sing like that!" she cried.

"Are you certain you are ready?"

In response, the princess opened her mouth and croaked forth a mighty frog song, so rich and emerald, so deep and powerful, that a thousand frogs rushed out of the forest to croak with her.

"Excellent, Princess! What a devoted student

you have been. All that remains is for you to recall the words of wisdom I spoke when first we met."

The princess closed her eyes, attempting to retrieve the words he had spoken, but she could not. "I feel that you told me something terribly important. It resides within me somewhere, but in a language I cannot understand. Please tell me again. I will try to remember this time."

"I will use different words, Princess," he said. "Perhaps these will be easier to remember: *There is nothing wrong with you. You are perfect as you are.*"

The princess pondered these words, and a faint flush of hope rose in her heart. For a moment, she believed this new truth about herself, but then the moment slipped away like a fish in a pond. "Young man," she said, bereft, "I am grateful for your kind words, but I know that there is something terribly wrong with me. Until I return home and sing before my suitors, I will not be perfect. On that day, my prince will choose me, and my life will be all that it should be."

"Your heart cannot receive the truth yet," he said sadly. "I cannot teach you more until it can. Good luck to you." He touched her on the cheek.

"Another long journey awaits you." He rose and helped her to her feet, then disappeared into the forest, singing a mournful song.

Five

There is nothing wrong with you. You are perfect as you are. These words accompanied the princess as she continued her journey but could find no home within her mind or heart. Once again, the young man faded from her memory. All that remained was a certainty that she had been condemned to inexplicable loneliness. Knowing that she could not yet return home, she sank to the ground and began to quietly weep.

"Others, too, have been denied gifts," said a high, eerie voice in her ear. "Others, too, have been shunned by the world. You are not alone."

The princess turned to see curled on a rock beside her an enormous snake with grey wrinkled skin.

As fearsome as the creature was, the princess took pains not to recoil or show her alarm, not wanting to seem disrespectful. She addressed the mighty snake, "How do you know my sorrow, Your Majesty?"

"I know many things," replied the Snake Queen.

"Perhaps then you know what is wrong with me!" the princess cried, forgetting her fear.

The Snake Queen stared at her. "I know that your race finds me repulsive and terrifying, and yet you have treated me with decency and respect. For that I will reward you." She began to hiss a light and lovely song. The longer the princess listened, the farther away seemed her sorrows.

"What an exquisite singing voice you have!" the princess cried. "It is like silver raindrops at my ear!"

"Others do not find it so," said the Snake Queen. "I am grateful for your admiration. We are very alike, kind princess. We do not find easy welcome in the world, although we mean no harm."

The princess felt happiness flooding her. To be understood by another creature! She dried her tears on her sleeve and rose from the ground.

"Would you like to learn my song?" asked the Snake Queen.

Five

"With pleasure!" cried the princess.

The Snake Queen uncoiled herself from the rock, raised her body high, and flicked her tongue at the princess's throat. "Sing!" she commanded.

The princess felt a strange stirring in her tongue. She opened her mouth to sing, expecting a croak, but instead a tiny hiss escaped, and then another. Before she knew it, she was hissing a lovely slithering sort of song. And although it was still not the voice which she had imagined for herself, it was nonetheless miraculous! Her body thrilled as she hissed, her voice growing stronger and stronger.

"S-s-s-s-cintillating!" praised the Snake Queen, joining her in song. Soon hundreds of snakes slithered to her ankles, swaying and hissing in harmony to her song. They hissed together for hours in a mighty chorus and danced a wild sinuous dance.

Finally, the princess stopped to catch her breath. "I can never thank you enough!" she said, barely able to speak for the excitement that arose in her throat. "Surely this voice is beautiful enough. I must return home at once to sing for my suitors!"

"Not yet, Princess," said the Snake Queen. "Have you forgotten your responsibility?"

The princess bowed her head in shame. "Forgive me. I would never shirk my duty. I forgot, for I have waited so long to experience love."

"There is another waiting," said the Snake Queen. "Listen carefully. You must practice your new voice with devotion as you go deeper into the forest. Soon you will meet someone who will give you good advice. You will be wise to follow it. And remember this:

> *Things are not what they may seem;*
> *A nightmare may become a dream.*
> *Within is fruit, without is rind.*
> *Who seems fearsome may be kind."*

And with these words, the Snake Queen scraped herself against a sharp rock and slipped out of her grey wrinkled skin. Her new silver body glittered like a star and illuminated the dark forest.

The princess fell to her knees and bowed her head.

"So that you should not forget me, take my old skin," the Snake Queen said. "Keep it with you always. It will protect you and save another's life."

The princess wrapped the featherlight snakeskin

around her neck like a scarf. "Thank you, Your Majesty. I will do all that you say."

With a strident hiss, the Snake Queen disappeared into the forest, and the princess continued her journey.

Six

The princess hissed her silvery song as she walked, her confidence in her new voice growing with each step. Although she fervently desired to return home to sing for her suitors, she continued her journey, considering the Snake Queen's enigmatic words and searching for her next teacher. Although she caught glimpses of animals here and there, and called to them, none would approach her.

Growing tired, she stopped to rest beneath a shady tree. At once the branches above her rustled with scurrying squirrels. "Run for your lives!" they chittered. "A strange and hideous serpent has entered our realm! Hear its silver song of death!"

The princess leaped to her feet, terrified, scanning the earth. "Where is this deadly serpent?" she called up into the tree. The squirrels only increased their frantic warnings and raced into the next tree. Mystified, the princess turned in a slow circle, searching the grass for movement, when a sudden horror overtook her. Was it she whom the animals feared? Had her singing caused them to flee? "I am your friend!" she cried into the forest, turning in all directions. But the only response was a trembling leaf or flower.

Despair fell upon her. She recalled the ladies of the court shivering as they discussed her heartlessness. Her snake song, which she had thought as lovely as silver bells, dried up in her throat. What if her suitors ran from her song as did the animals, feeling only fear and not love?

Then she heard in the distance an exquisite sound, so fascinating that in her curiosity she forgot her pain. She walked deeper into the forest. Soon she saw a young man sitting cross-legged on a rock, a strange animal in his lap. The enchanting sound abruptly ceased.

"Greetings, Princess," he said. "I have been waiting for you."

Six

"You seem to know me," she said. "But I do not know you."

"Have you really forgotten me, dear one?" He smiled and cradled the exotic animal.

The princess grew frightened that she could not remember one so obviously a friend.

"If I once knew you, I know you no longer," she said.

"Perhaps this will help." The young man threw back his head and burst into song, his voice as deep and rich as earth itself.

"Oh!" the princess cried. "I do remember you! You are the singing man. Two times now you have told me lovely stories about myself. I cannot recall your words precisely, although I know they brought me joy. Have you another story for me?"

In response, the young man began to stroke the animal. A lovely sound came from its body.

"Such beauty!" cried the princess. "That is the sound that drew me to you. We have nothing like it in my kingdom."

"You have never heard a lute before?"

"Lute?" the princess repeated. "I have never heard of such an animal."

He laughed. "It is not an animal—it is a musical instrument. It awakens feelings and memories and brings both sorrow and joy to the human heart." He bent over it again.

The princess began to weep. "Oh! That I could make such music!"

"What stops you?" He handed her the lute.

"I—I—stop myself," she said numbly.

"But why?" he inquired.

"I do not deserve such a gift, for I am hopelessly flawed."

"What an odd thing to think," he murmured. "Very, very odd." He began to play again.

The tantalizing music surrounded the princess, spinning, cradling, rocking her. She opened her arms, threw back her head, and hissed a mighty snake song, so high and wild, so fierce and strange, that a thousand snakes glided out of the forest to hiss with her.

Suddenly, she stopped. "I remember now what you told me."

The young man smiled. "The lute has done its work."

"Yes," she said, "a door within me swung open,

and I heard you say: *You are perfect just as you are.*" She sighed. "That is so clearly not true, though I am grateful," she said quickly, "for the kind intent behind your false words."

"False words? False words?" He gave a strange howling sound which scattered the snakes in all directions.

The princess jumped back. "Forgive me! I did not mean to anger you."

"I am not angry," he said, "only despairing." Grief flashed upon his face. "Too often I forget how human hearts, born soft and receptive, turn to stone from pain and are incapable of allowing love."

The princess placed her right hand upon her heart and began to cry. "Help me, please, my teacher! I do not wish to have a heart of stone!"

"No one wishes it, my dear."

He placed his hand beneath her chin and tilted her face to his. "I will tell you once more—three times are all I am allowed. You must remember this time."

"I will try, but your words flee from me, the way a dream does when I wake and try to recapture it."

"That is because you have only let my words

touch you. You must absorb them into your heart."

"But how can I absorb with a heart of stone?"

"How indeed?" he said and began to play upon the lute again. And as he played, he began to sing. The singing poured into her body like a rushing river, surrounding her heart, seeking out cracks in the stone, where it could enter. She was still young, and so there were many such entrances remaining.

She stood transfixed as he sang:

All are perfect; none are wrong.
Trust in me and in this song.
People grow in different ways.
Flowers bloom on different days.

All are perfect; none are wrong.
Nothing sad will last for long.
Some say life is but a dream;
Things are not what they may seem.

All are perfect; none are wrong.
Never fear you don't belong.
Time is young and time is old.
Trust the myst'ries to unfold.

Six

As she listened, she felt her heart grow soft and light within her chest. "Such a beautiful, beautiful song. I can almost believe the words."

He stopped singing and playing. "You must believe them. I can help you no more. Good luck to you, dearest princess." He disappeared into the forest.

Seven

Considering the young man's words carefully, the princess continued walking. It was a wonderful thing to entertain the lovely ideas in his song. Imagine a world where all could accept themselves as they were and where all could belong. She smiled, thinking about that world. But as she wandered farther and farther from the young man's presence, doubt grew within her once again. It was impossible to forget the disappointment on the king's and queen's faces, the fear in the eyes of the ladies of the court, and the discomfort of the suitors who had come to hear her sing. These unhappy images assailed her. How could she be perfect when so many thought otherwise? Somewhere there must be a potion or a spell to disenchant her. These dark thoughts wearied her, and she stopped to rest beneath a tree.

"Others, too, have sought unnecessary remedies," a voice growled in her ear.

The princess turned to see a huge wolf sitting beside her, his inscrutable eyes staring into the distance. "Unnecessary remedies?" she repeated. "What do you mean by these words, Wolf King?"

"I mean what I say and nothing more nor less." He turned to stare into her eyes. The princess saw that he was blind. She was filled with pity.

"Does your affliction grant you a deeper wisdom?" she asked. "Is that why your words are cryptic?"

"I am not afflicted," said the Wolf King.

The princess was afraid that she had angered him. "Are you not blind?" she asked.

"I am," said the Wolf King.

"But you do not wish to see?" she persisted.

"No. Nor do sighted wolves wish to become blind."

The princess struggled with this idea. Finally, she said, "It is not so for humans. If there is something wrong with us, we try everything to be made right."

"But who determines what is wrong?" asked the

Seven

Wolf King. "Or what is right?"

The princess pondered this.

"You cannot be cured," the Wolf King said.

"Then I will never be loved?" The princess burst into tears.

The Wolf King howled a mournful song. The longer he howled, the farther away seemed the princess's home and happiness.

"What a heartbreaking voice you have!" she cried. "It is like wind blowing through a graveyard."

The wolf stopped howling. "Others say the same. I am sorry to have broken your heart, but you cannot be cured, for there is nothing wrong with you. Like me, you are merely different. In my pack, I am the only blind wolf, yet I am the king. Consider what this means."

The princess stood, silent.

The Wolf King spoke again, "Would you like to learn my song? Or do you fear its sadness?"

"I must learn your song!" exclaimed the princess.

"Stand before me." The Wolf King raised himself and placed his great paws on her shoulders. His savage teeth and nose nuzzled her throat. "Sing!" he commanded.

The princess felt a stirring in her tongue. She opened her mouth to hiss her snake song, but instead a moaning howl escaped, and then another. Before she knew it, she was howling with the Wolf King. It was still not the voice that she had imagined for herself, but it was nonetheless miraculous! Her body pulsed with sorrow as she howled, her voice growing stronger and stronger.

"Magnificent!" cried the Wolf King.

Soon hundreds of wolves ran from the forest and howled with her. They howled together for hours in a melancholy chorus and danced a fierce dance.

"It is another miracle," the princess said at last. The sadness that arose in her throat made it difficult for her to speak. She found herself wondering about the person the Frog King and Snake Queen had spoken of—the one whose life she was to save with their gifts. Was that person filled with sadness as well?

"I cannot linger!" she cried. "Someone awaits my arrival. Have you advice for me?"

"Listen carefully," said the Wolf King. "You must practice your new voice with devotion as you go deeper into the forest. Your destination nears. And remember this:

Seven

Things are not what they may seem;
A nightmare may become a dream.
Night is Day and Slow is Swift.
What seems a curse may be a gift.

He gave a mighty howl and spat a tooth into her hand. "Carry this against evil," he said.

The princess opened the velvet bag she wore around her neck and placed the tooth beside the emerald eye.

"I am to meet evil then?" she asked, fear creeping over her body.

"There is no escaping it," said the Wolf King.

The princess shivered but had no thoughts of turning back. "Thank you, Your Majesty. I will do as you say."

With a final mighty howl, the Wolf King loped away, his pack behind him, and the princess set off deeper into the forest.

Eight

The princess continued along her path, and a strange sight she was—a beauty dressed in rags, croaking, hissing, and howling. Her spirit had been emboldened by her meeting with the Wolf King, and she now sang with whichever voice she pleased, enjoying them all. Soon she would return home and once again stand before her suitors and sing. Not every prince would find her animal songs to his liking, but the special one—the prince destined for her—would hear them with delight.

One day, as she was croaking a pleasing melody, the princess noticed with excitement that the path was at last coming to an end. She followed it to the place where it stopped, and then stood for a moment, hissing with curiosity. Stretched before her was a vast graveyard, studded with headstones as far as the eye could see, and in the distance, a dark castle. All the beauty of the forest ended here. The world ahead was grim and foreboding.

She howled softly. "Where does one go when one's path has ended?" Suddenly, a shadow of fear passed over her. "Is this then the beginning of the evil of which the Wolf King spoke?"

"Speak you of evil?" asked a voice at her ear.

The princess turned to see an ugly old wizard in a tattered cloak at her side. His ugliness was made more alarming by his friendly smile. "I've known you were coming for quite some time," he said. "The Princess with Four Voices was destined to arrive soon. I heard your grotesque animal songs growing louder."

"The Princess with Four Voices?" she wondered aloud.

"Yes," he answered. "There is a prophecy that a princess with four voices will destroy me and free the prince whom I have been holding prisoner. But you have only three voices." He cackled like an old

Eight

hen. "I used my magic to end your path before you could gain the final voice."

"But I have not come to destroy you or to rescue a prince," she responded. "I did not even know of your existence until this moment! I am on a journey to fulfil a personal responsibility so that I may return home. Please restore my path and allow me to pass. I must not linger."

"I will not," spoke the wizard. "Turn back at once! None may enter my magnificent garden!" He gestured to the desolate graveyard before them.

"Your garden?" The princess was filled with horror.

"Yes," the wizard replied. "My garden of death. All who attempt to thwart my plans and to rescue the prince are planted deep within the earth. You will be next if you do not turn back."

"But why?" asked the princess. "Why must you be so evil?"

"Because I take such pleasure in it," responded the wizard.

The princess shuddered. Never had she imagined such darkness existed in the world. Pain and suffering, grief and loneliness she knew. But this? She stumbled backward, shaking with fear.

"That's right," spoke the wizard soothingly. "Go back from whence you came."

Just then a bird's sharp cry tore the air. The princess remembered her duty. "I cannot," she spoke firmly, although she was still trembling. "I have a responsibility. If I leave it unfulfilled, I can never return home. I will be alone and unloved forever."

"That is not such a bad thing," the wizard replied. "I have lived that way all of my life. See how happy I am?"

"You do not seem happy to me," the princess said.

"Well, I am not actually alone," said the wizard, "only unloved." He crossed into his graveyard and shouted, "Prince of Dogs! Come here at once!"

From far away, behind a headstone in the far reaches of the cemetery, a young man stood and wiped the dirt from his knees. Weaving around the many graves, he walked toward the princess. She thought she had never seen a more beautiful face in her life, though a look of tremendous sorrow filled his eyes. She felt as if she were spinning. "You are as beguiling as the moon," she gasped. "In your eyes I see the beginning and end of my life."

"And you, dear princess," he countered, "are as

radiant as the sun. Your royal beauty shines from beneath your rags like a star in the midnight sky. I am heartbroken that you have come upon this unfortunate path. Please go back from whence you came. I have dug ninety-nine graves for ninety-nine princesses thus far. Do not let the hundredth be for you."

"That is enough!" spoke the wizard. "Return to your digging!"

"Goodbye, dear one," said the prince. "In your eyes I see wisdom, compassion, and strength. Lucky will be the one who earns your hand in marriage. Whatever unhappy accident guided you to this dark place, please turn back now." He shouldered his shovel and with a final regretful glance at the princess returned to the graveyard.

The wizard laughed. "Such a touching speech! It would move me to tears, were I capable of crying."

But he may as well have been speaking to a wall. After hearing the prince's noble words, the princess had fallen deeply in love. Surely his was the life she had been sent to save! "I did not come to destroy you," she said to the wizard, "but if that is the only way to free the prince, I will find a way to gain the fourth and final voice!"

The Princess Who Sang Like a Frog

"How?" The evil wizard barked a wicked laugh. "Your path is done. There is nowhere for you to go but back into the forest with your frogs and your snakes and your wolves. Sing your hideous songs for them! You have reached the end of your journey and have been found wanting. You have failed to do the one task ever asked of you, for you are imperfect, like all the other wretched humans who have come before you." He spread his arms wide to embrace his grave-yard. "My garden remains inviolate!" he shrieked, then disappeared in a puff of foul smoke.

Nine

The wizard's cruel parting words barely touched the princess, so overwhelmed was she by her encounter with the prince. Was the prophecy correct? Was she, in fact, the Princess with Four Voices destined to free him? If so, she was indeed imperfect; she had only three and did not know where to seek the fourth.

It was too much to bear.

An unfamiliar feeling began to roil inside of her, tormenting her spirit. The princess was no stranger to unpleasant feelings: shame and humiliation on her ill-fated debut; grief and despondency as one remedy after another had failed; and loneliness and despair over the past many months and hundreds of miles of travel. But these feelings were nothing compared to the whirlwind within her now. An enormous rage at the unfairness of her life grew within her. To have worked so long and so hard, and to still be denied! She raised her arms to the skies and croaked, hissed, and howled with anger that shook the leaves on the trees and made the branches tremble.

Suddenly, a shriek pierced the air. Two enormous birds, one silver and one golden, landed at the princess's feet. Both stood as tall as she.

Her animal songs abruptly ceased. "Your majesties!" breathed the princess. "Forgive my disrespectful outburst. Have I offended you?"

"Offended us? Most certainly not," said the silver bird. "Your singing attracted us. May we be of service?"

Swiftly, the princess told them her story. "Now the wizard has cut short my path," she cried, "and I cannot achieve the fourth voice!"

The golden bird spoke. "The wizard is a fool—as are all creatures bent on evil—to have forgotten that the path upward is never closed to those who ask for help." Both birds gazed into the sky.

"I did not realize that I was asking for help," the princess replied honestly. "I found myself

Nine

overwhelmed by a strange and sickening feeling, and something burst inside of me."

"That feeling is righteous anger," said the silver bird, "and it was so distressing that it took not one, but three, voices to express it."

"It is truly distressing," the princess said, still shaking from her outburst. "I do not enjoy this feeling at all."

"It is not meant to be enjoyed but to be used," said the golden bird. "You are destined to rescue the prince and to end the wizard's reign, but you cannot accomplish this without the power of your righteous anger."

The princess listened intently. "I will not fear my feelings, no matter how distressing, if they help rescue my beloved." To demonstrate, she threw back her head and croaked, hissed, and howled in anger.

"That is majestic music," said the birds. "You are ready now for the final voice." They tapped her throat with their enormous beaks. "Sing!" they commanded.

The princess closed her eyes and shrieked a deafening, shrill birdsong that brought her to her knees and split the sky asunder. A flock of silver and golden birds descended and hovered at her side to shriek with her. They shrieked together for hours in a mighty chorus, the birds weaving a complex dance around her, until suddenly the wizard appeared.

"Silence!" His harsh voice scattered the birds. "This singing must stop!" He reached for the princess's throat as if to strangle her, but as he touched the Snake Queen's skin, which she had wrapped around her neck, his hands burst into flame. He screamed and leaped backwards. "You will pay for this!" he snarled, shaking his smoldering palms with rage.

"She will pay for nothing but the prince's life," the golden bird rejoined.

The wizard scowled. "Then she must answer four riddles of my choosing. If she succeeds, I will surrender the prince."

"We will hold you to your promise," said the royal birds in unison. "We will be watching."

The wizard scowled more deeply.

"Remember our teachings," they told the princess and flew away.

Ten

"ctually," said the wizard with a cruel smile, "I am pleased that you have come. I have grown weary of torturing the prince and plan to execute him in a most painful fashion. Now I will have an audience for his gruesome death."

"Not if I can answer your riddles," said the princess.

"You will not be able to answer even my first riddle." The wizard scowled at his burned hands. "And the prince will die for his crime!"

"What crime?" the princess asked.

"The crime of his existence," said the wizard. "I do not like him. And since I am master here and can do as I please, I believe I am safe in saying that his death is assured."

As she considered his ugly words, righteous anger began to swirl inside the princess, strengthening her. "Ask me your riddles!" Her voice was hard and fierce. "I grow tired of you. If I answer them, you will set the prince free and leave us in peace."

"And if you fail?" asked the wizard. "What would you have me do with you?"

The princess was emboldened by the teachings of the royal birds. "I will not fail."

"It seems to me," the wizard said, "that you place too much faith in your final voice. To outwit me, you will need far greater magic than animal songs. Still, I enjoy a game—especially a game I am bound to win. Yes, let us play!" He rubbed his wounded hands together and cackled. "I shall ask you four riddles. If you fail to answer even one, I will kill the prince at once, and you will take his place in my dungeon. Do you agree to my rules?"

"I do," she said.

The wizard smiled. "Here is my first riddle: *What was I thinking last night as I gazed from my tower?* I will give you one day to solve this. And since you will not succeed, even in a million days, I will prepare to execute the prince tomorrow."

Ten

He vanished in a puff of foul smoke.

The princess trembled. How could she possibly answer such a riddle? How could anyone guess what was in another's mind? She settled cross-legged on the ground to think, croaking softly to calm herself. Soon her body grew quiet, her breathing even and peaceful, and several hours passed in deep silence. Many details of her travels passed through her mind, and she suddenly recalled the Frog King's memento. She reached into the velvet bag around her neck and extracted the emerald eye. It lay heavy and cool in her palm. She began to rub the stone between her thumb and fingers, and as she did the Frog King's words returned to her memory:

> *Things are not what they may seem;*
> *A nightmare may become a dream.*
> *What seems cold and made of stone*
> *May change its form by love alone.*

As she chanted the mysterious words, she continued to rub the stone, thinking of the prince and how greatly she longed to free him. Suddenly, the emerald melted into a pool of bright green and poured out of her hand.

"Bless you, Frog King!" she cried, leaping to her feet. She raced through the graveyard toward the wizard's castle, crying, "I know the answer to the first riddle!"

The wizard appeared before her. "You cannot possibly know the answer. You cannot know what was in my mind!"

"And yet I do," said the princess. "As you gazed from your tower last night, you thought this: *My power is so great I can reduce a stone to water!*"

And she croaked a victory song.

The wizard's face grew stormy. "You had help!" he shouted. "No one could answer that alone!" He stamped in an angry circle until he had calmed himself. "Very well, princess," he muttered darkly. "The first riddle was child's play. There are three more riddles, none of which you will be able to answer." His voice was severe, though truth be told, he had begun to feel frightened. His burned hands ached intolerably, stung as if by a thousand wasps.

"Ask your next riddle!" the princess demanded.

Eleven

The wizard threw open his arms. His shabby cloak flapped behind him. "Here is my second riddle: *What treasure of my childhood do I keep locked in a chest a thousand miles away?* You have one day in which to solve this!"

He vanished in a puff of foul smoke.

Although this riddle seemed twice as difficult as the first, the princess did not despair. She settled herself cross-legged in the graveyard to think, hissing softly to calm herself. Soon her body grew quiet, her breathing even and peaceful. Several hours passed in deep silence. Many details of her travels passed through her mind, and she suddenly recalled the Snake Queen's memento. She touched her neck and untied the fragile tissue. As she rubbed the snakeskin gently between her fingers, the Snake Queen's parting words returned to her memory:

> *Things are not what they may seem;*
> *A nightmare may become a dream.*
> *Within is fruit, without is rind.*
> *Who seems fearsome may be kind.*

As she chanted the mysterious words, she continued to rub the snakeskin, imagining the wizard bending over an old chest, rubbing his wounded hands together. As he opened the lid, his tattered cloak peeled away from his body and fell to the floor. The burned skin of his hands, too, peeled away, revealing fresh pink skin beneath. Then the wizard himself peeled away, and a boy stood before her, clutching a monkey doll dressed in a wizard's robe and holding a tiny wand.

"Bless you, Snake Queen!" the princess cried. She leaped to her feet. She had no time to spare. It had taken her a day of silent meditation, and the snakeskin had turned to powder beneath her

Eleven

fingers. She raced toward the wizard's castle, crying, "I know the answer to the second riddle!"

The wizard appeared and gazed at her scornfully. "That is impossible, for even I don't know the answer."

"What do you mean?" the princess asked.

"What I mean is that I have forgotten my childhood and therefore have no idea what I may have kept in a treasure chest." He cackled.

"I can refresh your memory," said the princess. "Inside the chest is a monkey doll dressed in a wizard's robe and holding a tiny wand."

And she hissed a victory song.

"No! No! It cannot be true!" the wizard cried in rage and pain. "Simian! Dearest monkey companion, how could I have forgotten you? You are the reason I am a wizard today, so taken was I with your cloak and wand. Oh, Simian, how I miss you!" And the wizard began to sob. "Listen to me," he begged the princess. "I am made powerless by my tears. At this moment, I am a good soul. Quick, before the evil within me resumes power, take this and free the prince!"

She reached for the key the wizard was pulling from a chain around his neck.

"Stop!" A shudder contorted the wizard's body.

"You are very clever, Princess. This forgotten memory you revived through trickery weakened me temporarily, but I am myself again. I will not lose this game."

When she saw the tears in his eyes, the princess felt a moment of compassion for him. Then she remembered all the evil for which he was responsible: the ninety-nine murdered princesses, the tortured prince. And those were only the deeds about which she knew! She called upon her righteous anger to strengthen her. "You are losing the game. I have solved the first two riddles and have no doubt that I can solve the final two."

Suddenly, the wizard staggered. Without a thought for his wickedness, the princess rushed to help him and accidentally touched his injured hands. He screamed with fury and pushed her away. "Don't touch me! Human touch sickens me!"

But where the princess's snakeskin-powdered hands had grazed his, the skin was swiftly healing.

Twelve

he wizard stared in shock at his hands. He
began to shake.

"It is a miracle!" cried the princess.

"It is an abomination!" shrieked the wizard.
"You have disturbed my body. I feel ill!"

"I do not understand," said the princess.

The wizard scowled. "What could you know of
the intricate miracle that is a wizard's body? Do you
think that I could not have healed my own hands
had I desired it?"

"But why would you not desire it?" asked the
princess.

"Are you asking me riddles now?" the wizard
taunted, having composed himself.

So amazed had she been by the transformation of the wizard's hands that the princess had forgotten her purpose. Now she cried, "Let us return to the game!"

"Yes, let us," said the wizard. "I long for an end to this tiresome exchange." He feigned a yawn, although he was, in fact, growing even more frightened of the princess. "Here is your third riddle: *What is the first thing I see every morning?* Think on that!" he cried in an unnaturally high voice. "You have one day!"

He vanished in a puff of foul smoke.

This riddle seemed twice as difficult as the last. The princess settled herself cross-legged on the ground outside the entrance to the wizard's castle to think, howling softly to calm herself. Soon her body grew quiet, her breathing even and peaceful, and several hours passed in deep silence. Many details of her travels passed through her mind, and she suddenly recalled the Wolf King's memento. She reached into the velvet bag around her neck and extracted the wolf's tooth. "I was to carry this against evil," she mused, rolling the tooth in her palm, and as she did the Wolf King's final words returned to her memory:

Twelve

Things are not what they may seem;
A nightmare may become a dream.
Night is Day and Slow is Swift;
What seems a curse may be a gift.

As she chanted the mysterious words, she continued to roll the tooth in her palm, imagining the wizard sleeping in a locked, windowless vault where none could disturb him or spy upon his wicked craft. She considered his potions and elixirs, his pouches of dried animals and jars of deadly plants, trying to decide which he would see first upon awakening. Suddenly, she felt a sharp bite on her hand. The Wolf King stood before her, his blind eyes wide open.

"Bless you, Wolf King!" she cried, leaping to her feet. She pushed open the door to the wizard's castle, just as her time was almost up. "Wizard!" she called out. "I know the answer to the third riddle!"

With a cracking sound, the wizard appeared before her. He trembled as he said, "The answer is unknowable, for I sleep in a locked vault with no windows, where none can spy on me."

"I know." The princess smiled. "That is why the first thing you see is always—and only—darkness."

And she howled a victory song.

The wizard was terrified and enraged beyond belief. Thrice he had been outwitted! At last he spoke. "I have until now asked you three of the easiest riddles in the world. A baby could have answered them. I was amusing myself because the final riddle is the only one that matters, and it is a riddle that none on earth can solve." He paused dramatically.

"If you are trying to frighten me," the princess said, "it will not work. Please get on with it."

"Why are you in such a hurry?" mused the wizard. "You will certainly fail, and I will then execute the prince and install you in my dungeon. How sad for both of you. If I had a heart, it would break. But alas, like you, I have no heart."

The wizard's mocking made no mark upon the princess. "Those words would once have tormented me," she said, "but now I know that they are false. The instant I saw the prince and heard his kind voice, I felt my heart bloom like a flower. He and I shall marry, and all will be as it should be. Let us end this game."

The wizard spoke then, in a quiet voice, "Here is the final riddle: *Why do I take such pleasure in doing evil?* You will have one day to solve this, dear Princess, although you will never find the answer."

Then he fell back into the recesses of his castle, trembling, for that was not the riddle he had intended to ask! The words had fallen from his tongue as if they had been spoken by someone else! He hurried to his bedchamber, locked the door, and pulled twenty blankets around himself to stop his shivering.

The final riddle sent a shock through the princess. Stunned, she stumbled out of the castle and into the graveyard. She fell to the ground beside the open grave the prince had been digging, shrieking softly to calm herself, but the riddle so disturbed her that she was unable to find the peace and stillness she needed to meditate upon it. "Royal Birds," she cried as she gazed into the sky, "the wizard has asked a riddle so dark that the answer may destroy me! And unlike the Frog King, the Snake Queen, and the Wolf King, you have left me no memento!"

At that moment, a mighty thunderstorm arose. The sky grew black. The wind howled. Lightning cracked. Icy rain drenched the princess. She did not hear the flapping wings of the enormous birds who came to rest at her feet. "Climb upon my back, princess," the silver bird sang, "for you must travel to another world to find that which you seek."

Thirteen

But let us go back in time. . . .

In the early evening of the day he had met the princess, the prince had seen the flock of silver and golden birds descending and heard the glorious uplifting singing, followed by the wizard's angry shouting. He wanted to rush to the sound, but the wizard had chained him to his spot before the hundredth grave. He could move no further than a few steps in any direction, although nothing visibly seemed to detain him. The wizard's methods of torture were frequently of this sort. They had driven the prince to near madness. Years of captivity had so diminished his spirit that he had ceased trying to escape or even to hope that the wizard would one day release him.

But with the princess's arrival, the prince felt renewed faith. The sight of her face and the sound of her voice bolstered his courage and strengthened his heart. For the first time in years, he considered the possibility of freedom.

That night the wizard had been in an even fouler mood than usual when he ushered the prince to his dungeon. He had even forgotten to taunt him with his usual cruel words. And although he tried to hide his hands under the voluminous sleeves of his cloak, the prince saw the wizard's charred fingers as he opened the door of his cell.

For the next three days, the wizard did not arrive to summon the prince for his grave-digging duty nor to torture him in any way. The prince spent this unaccustomed leisure time daydreaming about the princess.

On the third night, a mighty storm battered the grimy skylight window of his dungeon, and the prince dreamed that he flew upon a great golden bird, high above the wizard's dreary graveyard. The princess flew beside him upon a magnificent silver bird. This splendid dream fed his awakening heart, which had been pricked to life by the princess's visit, and he awoke invigorated and fiercely impatient to once and for all escape the wizard's clutches.

He pounded the blood-stained walls and scraped the filthy floor strewn with human bones and rusted weapons, searching for a secret door or tunnel. Of course, he had done these things many fruitless times over the long years. Yet he felt a strange and curious hopefulness. His heart began to lighten, and he surprised himself by croaking an odd little melody as he searched. What had become of his voice after years of never lifting it in song! He sounded like a frog! But he continued to croak, his thoughts turning again and again to the beautiful princess. He could not bear the thought that she, too, would be buried in the wizard's graveyard. He must find a way out. He must save her! His croaking song grew stronger.

"Good prince, you have finally awoken! Rejoice!" croaked a voice at his feet.

The prince stared down at an impossibly large frog.

"Frog King!" he exclaimed. "Have I disturbed

your sleep with my pounding and scraping? You have never visited me before."

"You have never summoned me before," croaked the Frog King. "Your song drew me here."

"For that I am grateful," spoke the prince. "I have nearly died of loneliness! Forgive me if I am not good company at the moment. I am desperate to escape this dungeon and to rescue a beautiful princess from the wizard's evil designs."

"I will help you," croaked the Frog King. "But know this: the princess has departed on a quest to save your life. She must answer the most diabolical riddle ever devised. Should she succeed, the wizard's power will evaporate, and you will both gain your freedom. But you must help her discover the answer."

"How can I possibly help?" cried the prince. "I am locked in this miserable dungeon and can't even help myself!"

"But you can," croaked the Frog King. "Look around your home. How can you think in this vile place? To discover the riddle's solution, you must first sweep your floor."

"Sweep my floor?" said the prince with a bitter laugh. "What help can come from sweeping my floor?"

Thirteen

"Trust me when I tell you that no escape will be possible until you have done what I ask." The Frog King issued a mighty croak. "Bring the prince a broom!" Lo and behold, there came hopping to the cell door hundreds of frogs bearing upon their glistening backs a sturdy broom, which the prince pulled through the bars of his cell.

"Frog King, although your request seems strange, I will do as you ask. Yours is the first kind voice, besides the princess's, I have heard in years."

"Good luck to you, Prince!" The Frog King hopped through the bars of the cell and disappeared with his army, and the prince set to work sweeping the filthy dungeon floor. The longer he swept, the larger the floor seemed. Human bones, blood-stained shackles and chains, evidence of the wizard's gruesome deeds, piled up at the door of his cell. After hours of backbreaking work, the floor, though still grimy and blood-stained, had been swept bare.

In the far corner the prince spied something gleaming. One hand still on the broom, he plucked from the floor a golden ring covered with dust and grime. He polished it on his shirt. The star-shaped ruby surrounded by sapphires stirred a vague memory. He put the ring in his pocket.

When he turned, he saw to his amazement that the refuse near the cell door had vanished, and that the human bones had been neatly arranged into the skeleton of a man. The prince gazed at the skeleton. His finger went to the ring in his pocket, and he had an urge to place it on the left ring finger-bone of the skeleton, which he did. Then he carefully rearranged the skeleton, one bone at a time, upon his cot. After completing his work, he fell deeply asleep on the dungeon floor.

Fourteen

T he prince awoke from a dream that he was flying through the world on a golden bird. "Would that I could one day fly from this prison!" he cried into the emptiness of his cell. Then the events of the previous day rushed back—the croaking song, the visit from the Frog King, the hours of work sweeping the filthy floor. And the skeleton! He jumped to his feet to gaze at the bony frame lying on his cot. Instead of horrifying him, the skeleton eased his loneliness. He touched the fingerbone upon which he had placed the ring.

This unaccustomed peace lasted only a moment. He was no closer to escaping nor to rescuing the princess. He surveyed his cell. What good had come from sweeping his floor? He opened his mouth to croak, hoping to summon the Frog King again. But instead of a croak, a hiss emerged, and then another. Soon he found himself whistling a strange new song. Within moments, an enormous snake glided through the bars of his cell and fixed her eyes upon him.

Although his song dried up in his throat, the prince stood tall and faced the serpent. "What evil will you do me today?" he asked bravely. "Wrap yourself around my neck and choke me while the wizard laughs? Sink your fangs into my hands and feet?"

"I am no minion of the wizard's!" hissed the Snake Queen. "Can you not recognize a friend?"

The prince then saw the kindness in the serpent's gaze. "Forgive me. I am not myself and have not been for many years."

"No apologies, dear Prince," said the Snake Queen. "I know what you have suffered. Only the most stalwart of men could face me so bravely."

"I welcome your compassion," said the prince humbly, "as well as your guidance. My princess is engaged in a dangerous battle of wits with the wizard. I must go to her at once!"

Fourteen

"I see that you have begun the task assigned you by the Frog King." The serpent observed his cell. "Yet you are only halfway through the floor-cleaning. It is still grimy and blood-stained. You cannot help your princess until you have washed your floor."

Again, the floor! The prince feared he had gone mad over his years of incarceration. "Forgive my impatience, but how can washing my floor help my princess answer a riddle?"

"Are you privy to all the mysteries of the world?" The Snake Queen's voice grew severe. "If you already know how to help your princess, why did you summon me?"

Ashamed, the prince said, "Please pardon my disrespect. It is only that it seems unnecessary."

"Your princess followed instructions without question. She did not believe that she knew better than others. Follow her example!" The Snake Queen rose to her full height. "The prince needs water!" she hissed.

Immediately hundreds of snakes came gliding into his cell. Each snake poured silvery water from its mouth onto the floor of the dungeon. Then they wriggled away, scraping off their skins on the iron bars as they left.

The prince stared dumbfounded at the wet floor and the snakeskins.

"Do as you are told!" the Snake Queen hissed. She glided away.

The prince stood for a moment, wondering if this were some new torture the wizard had devised, when a sharp cry caught his attention. He gazed upwards and saw a golden bird poised on the sill of the dungeon's high window. Recalling the golden bird from his dream, he at once fell to his knees, grabbing handfuls of the rough skins and scrubbing fiercely at the floor as he whistled a snake song.

Soon intricate mosaic tiles emerged beneath the grime and blood. The tiles told a story, and the prince found himself drawn into the images as he scrubbed. The first tile showed a small boy in a dark room. Beneath it were the words: *Once upon a time, a boy lived in a joyless home.*

The prince traced the image of the boy with his fingers, and then slowly read the accompanying words aloud. Prior to his capture by the wizard, books had been among his most-beloved possessions. He often thought he could have borne his captivity easier had he access to a library, but the wizard had deprived him of this pleasure, too, torturing him by placing books filled with blank pages in his cell. It was difficult, after so long without reading, for the prince to even comprehend the words beneath the image. He repeated them several times, until their meaning became clear. Who was this boy? Why was his home joyless and dark?

Desperate for more of the story, the prince scrubbed the blood and grime from the next tile, which depicted a man standing over a grave. A crying baby lay on the earth beside him. Beneath this tile were the words: *His mother had died giving birth to him. His heartbroken father blamed him for her death.*

The prince stared for a long time at this picture. His heart ached for the father who had lost his wife but even more so for the motherless baby. Curiosity followed sympathy—the prince had to know what happened next! He grabbed another snakeskin and scrubbed the next image. This tile depicted the man, rage on his face, raising his hand to the boy. The accompanying words: *As the boy grew older, his father beat him or ignored him for days at a time.*

How could a father treat his son like this? The

prince's kind heart, despite the years of cruelty by the evil wizard, felt the poor unloved boy's pain. His own father—the king—had never treated him with anything but kindness. How the prince missed his father! And his beautiful mother! Oh, the pain of memory! This story he was reading— on a dungeon floor—returned his childhood to him. He fought to hold back tears as his memories threatened to overwhelm him.

He took a deep breath and scrubbed the next tile. It portrayed a boy sitting in a graveyard, clutching something to his heart. The words beneath said: *For sympathy and companionship, the boy turned to a monkey doll dressed as a wizard. He had found the doll beside his mother's gravestone.*

The prince continued to scrub the floor, releasing the final images. On the next tile, a much older boy stood near a window, his mouth hard and stern. The words beneath said: *With each passing year the gentleness was erased from the boy's features and the trust and kindness from his eyes.*

The prince's heart ached as he read these words. The boy had lived a loveless life, with nothing but a doll for company. Of course, he had lost his innocence.

Fourteen

Compassion for the boy washed over the prince as he scrubbed the next tile. On this one a young man walked away from a dark house. The words beneath the image: *The boy grew to manhood. He put away his childhood toys and set off into the world.*

The prince brightened. Perhaps the young man would meet someone on his travels, a friend, who would make his life happier. He scrubbed impatiently at the next tile, revealing an image of an ugly old man in a black cloak. Underneath it were the words: *The young man met a master crueler than his father, who transformed him into an evil wizard.* At these words, the prince's breath caught in his throat. Suddenly, he did not want to know more of this story.

The golden bird at the high window sang out: "Fear not. Your future will be better than your past. Follow your curiosity."

The prince took a deep breath, picked up one of the remaining snakeskins, and scrubbed the next tile. Upon it he saw a beautiful girl crying in her bed, mournfully rubbing her throat. No words accompanied the image. Curious, the prince scrubbed the next tile, upon which the same girl, older, danced in a forest with frogs, snakes, and wolves. Fiercely, he scrubbed the final tile, which revealed a young woman standing before the ugly old man in the black cloak. "It is my princess!" he gasped.

Suddenly, exhaustion set upon him, and he fell into a deep sleep on the dungeon floor. When he awoke, the images had vanished. He rubbed his eyes in disbelief. The floor now shone like a mirror, and by some miracle, the skylight, covered for centuries with grime, was bright and clear. A brilliant golden sun poured into the dungeon. In fact, it could barely be called a dungeon now. The prince gazed with wonder at the magnificent light. For the first time in years a quiet thrill of hope teased his spirit. But what pleasure could he take in his surroundings when his princess was still in danger and when he still could not escape and help her solve the diabolical riddle?

An object gleaming on the floor caught the prince's eye. It was a locket. He carefully pried it open and found a curling lock of hair that looked exactly like his mother's. Compelled by the same urge that had made him place the ring on the skeleton's finger-bone, he knelt before the cot and placed the locket around the skeleton's neck.

Fifteen

The prince stood now and bathed in the golden warmth streaming from the skylight, feeling stronger than he had in years. He strode to the cell door and began to work at the lock with renewed vigor. As he labored, he opened his mouth to hiss, hoping that the Snake Queen might provide further instruction, but instead of a hiss, a moaning growl escaped, and then another. Soon he was howling a mournful song. All the sorrows he had ever suffered filled his heart—the loss of his father and mother, his imprisonment and torture by the wizard, and now a sharp new pain that he could not rescue the princess, with whom he had fallen deeply in love.

He had not cried in years—not since the first lonely, terrifying weeks in the dungeon. To withstand the wizard's torments, he had hidden his grief so deeply that he had almost forgotten its existence. Now, his sadness exploded in blinding tears and howls of pain, so that he did not see nor hear the enormous wolf loping to his cell door. The wolf lay down and rested his head on his paws as he waited quietly for the prince to finish weeping.

Finally, the prince noticed his visitor. He wiped his eyes on his filthy shirt. "Forgive me, Wolf King, for this embarrassing display. I am not a weak man, but I have suffered much."

"I, too," said the Wolf King, "have experienced much grief in my life. I would like to cry with you." He raised himself to his feet, threw back his shaggy head, and howled a melancholy song.

The wolf's pain tore through the prince's body and soul. He dropped to his knees and howled in companionship. Their mournful duet went on for hours. Suddenly, all went quiet.

The prince shook himself, like a wolf, and gazed into the Wolf King's blind eyes.

"It is right and proper to express grief," spoke

the Wolf King. "You cannot be bold and brave and do good work in the world if you fear the depths of your heart."

"I know you are right," said the prince, astounded. "This morning, when the glorious sunlight warmed my body, I grew strong enough to let my heart speak. I am ready now for a life outside of these bars. Tell me how to rescue my princess."

Gesturing to the freshly-scrubbed floor, the Wolf King said, "You have perfected your home. You need now to perfect your appearance. You cannot set off to rescue your princess dressed in filthy rags."

The prince remembered the Snake Queen's words about following instructions without question. He gazed down at his torn, dirty clothing and responded, "You are right. I am not properly attired."

"The prince needs new clothes!" barked the Wolf King.

Hardly had he spoken when a pack of wolves swarmed the dungeon door, each carrying in its mouth a ball of thread or a packet of needles, or scissors, or measuring sticks, or bolts of precious fabric, passing their gifts one at a time through the bars of the cell door, and then loping away.

"Prepare yourself for the world!" exclaimed the Wolf King.

He disappeared.

The prince set to work at once, unrolling bolts of fabric, measuring, cutting, stitching. All the while he howled a wolf song. Low and rich, wild and mournful, his voice echoed in the enormous dungeon. When he had finished his own princely vestments, he found himself cutting a magnificent cloak fit for a king.

Finally, the exhausted prince finished. As he lifted the cloak to admire his handiwork, he discovered beneath it a golden crown set with rubies and sapphires. Without a second thought, he placed the crown on the skeleton's head, and then fell asleep on the shining floor.

As he slept, the prince dreamed that a golden bird carried him in the dark of night to a faraway land and left him in a pond. While the prince lay in the water, as helpless and blind as a newborn, two kind hands bathed him and anointed him with oil. A woman's tender voice cried, "My son! My son! How I love you!" With each utterance of this blessed incantation, the prince's body grew stronger,

Fifteen

until all the wounds inflicted by the wizard over the years were healed.

When he at last awoke, the prince found himself warm, clean, and garbed in rich robes. The skeleton and the cot had vanished. Standing over him was a splendidly dressed king, a golden crown set with rubies and sapphires upon his head. "Come, my son," said the king. "It is your wedding day."

Sixteen

And what was the wizard doing during the mighty storm? Truth be told, he had grown weaker each day since the arrival of the princess and now lay sobbing and shivering beneath his twenty blankets. Where the princess had touched his wounded hands, the skin was nearly restored. His body felt strange and unfamiliar.

To add to his distress, he ached with loneliness for Simian, his long-ago companion. After how many brutal beatings by his father had he cried himself to sleep with Simian's small body pressed beneath his chin? How many lonely, motherless afternoons had been brightened by the monkey doll's presence? The more that he remembered of his childhood, the greater grew the wizard's desire to have Simian by his side once again. He threw off his twenty blankets and hurried about his room, collecting ingredients for a most powerful spell.

When he had placed a careful assortment of items—an emerald, a snakeskin, a wolf's tooth, and a bird's wing—into a large black metal pot, he incanted magic words so dark and secret I cannot repeat them here. And as he chanted, stirring his strange brew, the wizard closed his eyes and held the image of Simian fast in his mind.

A loud crack broke his concentration. The wizard's eyes flew open, and he beheld not a monkey doll but a real monkey. A real monkey wizard! The creature was dressed in a faded purple cloak. He turned his deep golden eyes on the wizard and smiled.

"Where is my doll!" the wizard bellowed. "You are not Simian! You are alive! Return from whence you have come!"

"I am Simian, good Zadri," the monkey replied.

Zadri. Upon hearing his own name spoken for the first time in many years, the wizard felt an icy sword stab him to the core.

"Your brilliant wizardry has made me real!" the

monkey continued. "Thank you, old friend. Long have I waited in the chest of our childhood home, yearning for your companionship, and you have at last rescued me. How old you have grown!" The monkey surveyed the wizard. "Tell me, dear good Zadri, all the glorious and noble things you have done with your powers. I cannot wait to hear! Remember how you promised to care for the sick and needy, to love all creatures, to help whenever you could, and to never harm?" The monkey's eyes glazed with tears. "You were such a loving boy. I know you have become a great and kind wizard, helper of men and women, children and animals. Come, show me your castle and the evidence of your good deeds."

Zadri froze in mute horror. Had he really said those things when he was a child? When had he become so evil? How could he tell his dearest companion what he had become? A wild and clever plan, born of desperation, came to the wizard's mind.

"Dearest Simian, loving companion of my childhood and dearer to my heart than my own self," he said in an unfamiliar voice. "A wearying illness has overcome me, and I feel quite feeble. I have called you forth to comfort me. If you will rest with me beneath my twenty blankets for a few hours, then I will show you my kingdom."

The monkey happily clambered into the bed, burrowing under the blankets and clinging to Zadri. He had not noticed the wizard's haggard cruel appearance nor the shabby room in which he slept. Such is love. It sees what is true and not what is false, and strange as it may seem, in the deepest recesses of the wizard's heart, a spark of goodness remained, waiting for even the smallest breeze to awaken its fire.

Zadri sank into the pillows. Tears streamed from his eyes as he felt the weight of Simian curled beneath his chin as in days of yore. Tears for all the good he could have done but did not. Tears for all the cruel and evil things he had done.

He felt his eyes grow heavy. When he arose, he would begin the difficult work of putting his wild and clever plan into effect. But first, first.... Nestled in the pillows, with the monkey's tiny heart beating next to his, he felt a peace he had not known since childhood. Just before he fell into sleep, he noticed the strangest thing: a skylight had appeared in the ceiling of his dark room, and he could see a beautiful full moon glowing above his chamber.

Seventeen

When Simian awoke the next morning, he found Zadri seated beside him. "Now that you are awake—and alive—you must eat," Zadri said. He waved his wand, and fruits and nuts of all colors, sizes, and shapes appeared on a silver platter. Simian bit into each fruit and nut with curiosity and delight, his pleasure in eating growing by the moment. He ate until he could eat no more, then stretched his new body from head to toe, and stared with great interest at his surroundings. "Oh, Zadri," he sighed. "How beautiful are your chambers!"

And they were.

Early that morning, after incanting a spell that had shaken him to the root of his evil being, the wizard had transformed his dismal bedroom into a majestic suite. Except for one dark spot on the ceiling, which had stubbornly resisted his spell, his chambers were immaculate. Gleaming tiles of silver and gold covered the floors. Magnificent tapestries hung from sunny walls. A wash of brilliance poured through the skylight. A canopy spattered with stars crowned Zadri's bed. Above his pillow swayed a monkey-sized hammock spun of fine gold. In Simian's wildest dreams he could not have imagined such a beautiful home. He had been so amazed at finding himself alive and reunited with his best friend the previous night that he had not noticed any of this.

Simian jumped into his golden hammock and then out onto the wizard's bed and then back into the hammock until he tired of this game. Then with a glint in his eye, he sprang onto the wizard's right shoulder. Zadri gave a hoarse laugh. It sounded horrible and false to his ears. He said quickly, "I am still recovering, Simian. It hurts to laugh."

"I am sorry that you have not been well, my friend," said Simian. He sprang back to his hammock. "What is the nature of your illness?"

Seventeen

Zadri chose his words. "I have not been myself lately."

"Yes, the illness has changed you," said Simian.

"A few nights of rest are all I need," said Zadri. "Now that you are here, I feel myself recovering."

"I am glad that you are feeling better," said Simian. "I am eager to see the rest of your castle and your realm. May we stroll outdoors? I have not felt a breeze for years nor smelled the fresh air."

Zadri was filled with a creeping horror. "I am too weak yet for exercise." The spell he had cast at dawn had so depleted his energy that he had none left to transform the remainder of his castle nor the barren graveyard surrounding it. Until he could reinvigorate his powers, he needed to restrain Simian's curiosity and keep him away from the evidence of his evil deeds. "I need to lie down for a few moments," he said.

"Of course, my friend," said Simian. "I am at your service. Let us both have a nap. I have never eaten before, and it has tired me." He lay in his hammock, hands intertwined behind his head, and fell into a sound sleep.

Zadri crawled into his gorgeous new bed and lay

on his back, momentarily safe from fear. Everything was going according to plan. If he could maintain the fiction of his illness, he could keep the monkey's love and admiration. In truth, he did feel rather weak and odd. Was he ill? Had he not been himself?

As Zadri comforted himself with these thoughts, a shadow on the ceiling made his blood run cold. Dangling from a blood-stained web near the skylight, an enormous spider spun and twirled. Zadri's heart sank when he saw it. This was the dark spot, the imperfection that had resisted his most powerful transformational spell. There was something so evil about the spider that Zadri felt choked inside. It seemed a picture of his soul. Of course, he had been fooling himself. He could not blame his wicked past on an illness. He was doomed, and this spider was proof. It was only a matter of time until Simian learned the awful truth, but he hoped for a few more days to enjoy the warmth of the little creature's love.

Eighteen

When Zadri awoke, he found Simian sitting beside his pillow. "You look much better, Zadri." The monkey commenced to chatter. "Every hour I feel more gratitude and wonder at how you were able to bring me to life. Not every wizard has the power to do such a thing. How did you accomplish it?"

Zadri had no answer. It was an accident—one he could never repeat—but he was too fearful of losing Simian's admiration to admit it. "I work in mysterious ways," he said solemnly. "I cannot explain my gifts." As he spoke these words, he glanced at the ceiling. The massive spider was lowering itself on a silken string above Simian's head. Without a thought, Zadri cried, "That is not true, Simian!"

The spider paused in its descent.

"What is not true?" asked the monkey.

Zadri hung his head. "I do not know how you were brought to life. It was. . . ." He started to say it was an accident, but different words fell from his tongue. "It was the greatest gift I have ever been given." Tears stung his eyes and his breath caught in his throat as he realized that he had spoken the truth.

"It was my greatest gift as well!" cried Simian. "We must give thanks to your benefactor. Who is it?"

"I am ashamed to say that I do not know," said Zadri. He felt confused. "I do not know whom to thank."

"Then we shall give thanks to Life Itself!" Simian fell to his knees and bowed his head, clasping his hands tightly, as if in prayer. Zadri gasped. He had never knelt except when his cruel father had beat him. Nor since his childhood had he clasped his hands in prayer. No help had come to him during those times, so he had ceased to pray. As if in a spell, the wizard dropped to his old knees,

Eighteen

his bones creaking in protest. Although he did not notice, his hands had healed. They were clean and unwrinkled, like the hands of a boy. His new hands met easily in front of his chest, and he joined the monkey in gratitude.

"Thank you, Life. Thank you for giving yourself to Simian. Thank you for returning joy and happiness to me. How may I thank you in return?" These unaccustomed words took Zadri's breath away.

Suddenly, he found himself rising from the floor with ease and walking to his workbench. His hands moved of their own accord—or so it seemed—opening jars, pouring liquids, and waving his wand in complicated patterns, until—poof!—a tiny silver tub filled with fragrant water materialized on the workbench.

"What is that?" Simian asked.

Zadri was staring in wonder at his creation. He was not sure how he had done it. "It is a bathtub," he said.

"But what is it for?" Simian said. "It is far too small for you."

Yes, what is it for? Zadri asked himself, and then he spoke: "Simian, you have been locked in a chest for years and smell musty. You must bathe."

How strange that I should say this, Zadri thought, I who have not bathed in years.

Simian tried to leap back into his hammock, but the wizard held him fast by his long tail. "A bath you must have."

"I have never been immersed in water," said Simian fearfully.

"That is because you were only a doll," said Zadri. "But now you are real. Real animals clean and groom themselves."

He placed Simian at the edge of the fragrant tub. Simian sniffed the water, then dipped his tail in to test it.

"All right, old friend," Simian said finally, "I will get into this tub on one condition—you must also take a bath."

Zadri froze. Bathe? He? It would be terribly dangerous! But suddenly, more than he had ever wanted anything, Zadri wanted to take a bath. He wanted to be clean and young and new again. He wanted to begin a life of goodness, such as he had promised Simian when he was a child. But what of all the evil he had wrought? How would he pay for that? He could no longer remember what had

Eighteen

possessed him to begin his life of darkness, and he could not remember the last time, if ever, that he had felt real pleasure in his work.

"Will you make yourself a bathtub?" Simian interrupted the wizard's grim thoughts.

Zadri stared at his wand and noticed his new hands for the first time. He began to shake. Such a transformation was unthinkable! He felt a great fear.

"I—I can't." The wizard placed his wand on his workbench and burst into tears.

Nineteen

ear Zadri, what is wrong?" Simian jumped
to the wizard's shoulder and threw his
arms around his neck. "Why do you cry? Is
it your sickness?"

"Simian, you cannot love me!" howled Zadri
through his tears. "I am a wicked, wicked wizard
who has wrought terrible crimes in the world. You
are better off as a doll locked in a chest than a friend
to such an evil person!"

"Zadri, what do you mean by this wild talk?"
The monkey hugged the wizard tightly.

"Your friend is in dire need of a bath," said a
voice behind him. Simian spun around. He saw no
one, but on the floor beside the workbench stood an

ornate golden and silver tub, just like Simian's, but large enough for a man.

Zadri's eyes widened in shock and fear, and he began to tremble.

Simian was delighted. "Look, Zadri! Certainly this bath is magical and will make you feel better. Let us both bathe."

Again, Zadri's hands moved of their own accord, although not against his will, and loosened his robe. He stepped into the tub and lowered his old, wicked body into the water, which smelled like roses. The shock took his breath away. How many years ago had he vowed to never feel purifying water on his body? The bathwater had turned as black as sludge the moment he climbed into the tub, but it magically renewed itself. By the third renewal, Zadri's body turned the water only a dark grey. By the tenth, the water remained clear. Zadri felt as light as a feather.

Part of him could not believe this was happening—that he was taking a bath—but another part of him felt calm, as if his years of evil had been only a terrible mistake, a detour from the true path of his life. All Zadri had been and known was dissolving.

Nineteen

At last he called out, "All right, Simian. It is your turn."

Simian stepped out of his robe. Squeezing shut his eyes and holding his nose, he sprang into the tub. What a surprise! He found that he loved the feel of water on his body. He swam around and around until he grew tired, and then climbed out and shook himself dry.

"Zadri!" he cried, as his delighted eyes fell upon an extraordinary gift. On the workbench, in place of his faded, threadbare cloak, lay a magnificent purple robe. Simian slipped it on with tremendous excitement. He felt as regal as a king. His eyes fell upon a wizard's hat spun with silver and gold threads. He placed it on his head. Then he saw a silver wand lying upon a book called *Good Magic for Good Monkeys*. Simian's new heart could hardly hold this happiness. He leaped to the edge of the wizard's tub and began chattering wildly, thanking him again and again.

But Zadri barely heard him, so wildly was his heart pounding. Who had created these gifts? And what now would Simian think of the shabbiness of his own clothing compared to the creature's new apparel? Shame overwhelmed him. He hurried to whisper an incantation, when he saw hanging in the air before him a gorgeous robe, a wizard's hat, and a golden wand. Reeling with curiosity and wonder, Zadri stared at the gifts, certain he did not deserve them. But again, his body moved without conscious effort, and he reached for the shimmering garment, pulling it around himself. Peering into the mirror, he donned his new hat. His grey tangled beard turned shiny and black, and the weariness and pain disappeared from his face.

He plucked the golden wand from the air and waved it. A book appeared. On the cover were the words *A Wizard's Book of Magic for Good and Loving Purposes*. Zadri felt a wild tug at his heart, and then a great peace came over him.

"Zadri," Simian sang with delight. "Let us go outside and greet your friends. They will be overjoyed to see that you have recovered."

Zadri hesitated. He gazed at the ceiling, searching for the wicked spider. A lovely blue butterfly hovered now near the skylight.

"Come!" he said brightly to Simian. "It is time for you to know the truth." And to himself Zadri whispered: Let it be done.

Twenty

Through wild cold rain, through ice and snow, through burning sunshine, the princess flew upon the backs of the royal birds, who took turns carrying her. Memories of the prince and the wizard grew dim. The music of the frogs, the snakes, the wolves, and the birds was soon forgotten, and the problem of singing ceased to trouble her. After many weeks, the princess no longer remembered her former life. The blinding sun and stinging rain assaulted her eyes. The brutal wind and bitter snow whistled about her ears and tore at her throat. She lay like a wraith, blind, deaf, and dumb, upon the bird's back, until one day she felt a jolt and then stillness. Finally, the birds had come to rest.

With great effort, the princess opened her eyes. Through the haze, she saw that she had been deposited in a nest of golden fibers in the branches of a silver tree. Beside her lay a strange wooden object. Overwhelmed by the journey, she fell asleep.

The princess lived in this huge golden bowl for a very long while, occasionally raising herself on tiptoe to peer over the edge. When she was hungry, she opened her mouth wide like a greedy fledgling, and the royal birds fed her bits of golden fruit and sap from the silver tree. She grew strong and vibrant again, and her mind and heart opened like flowers and filled with light. When she was tired, she slept deeply beneath a silver and gold feather blanket, content to pass her life in this glorious home in which all needs were met.

But one night she awoke, strangely restless. She rose from her feathered bed, and in the darkness, stumbled over the wooden object. A lovely sound rang out. It hung in the air and grew louder and louder, filling her body, as if it were food or drink. A rolling sensation overtook her. She began to spin in dizzying circles, bumping against the sides of her nest. As she whirled and twirled, her memories began to return, slowly at first, and then in a barrage, a storm, a frightening jumble of animals, forests, a graveyard, a castle, an ugly old man, and finally, the face of the beautiful prince.

"My love!" she cried. Her throat pained her, so long had it been since she had spoken. "I have not forsaken you!" And with these words, the princess remembered why she had come to this golden bowl on a silver tree in a faraway land.

The royal birds swept into the nest. "You once said that the birds had given you no memento," spoke the Bird King, stretching forth a wing to touch the wooden object. "Here now is our gift to you."

The princess stared at it for a long time. "I have seen this object before, but I have forgotten its purpose." She reached for it and moved her hands over its surface. The ringing sound filled the air again and made her tremble. She sat back upon her bed, cradling the object and rocking back and forth, allowing the sound to enter her body.

After a long time, she grew still. "It is called a lute. It is a tool of memory. It can break one's heart and heal it as well. A singing man offered it to me long ago, but I would not take it. I did not feel worthy of such a gift."

"Many receive unexpected gifts," said the Bird Queen, "not as payment for one's worth but as an expression of the giver's generosity."

The princess smiled. "I will receive your gift with gratitude, Your Majesties, and also ask that you return me to my prince. His life is in my hands."

"Have you the answer to the wizard's final riddle?" the Bird Queen continued. "It was revealed to you in many ways during your travels. You need only remember what you were told."

"Everything is mixed up in my head and my heart," said the princess. "I met many royal animals who spoke odd poetry. But that is all I can recall."

"Perhaps if you sing with the lute," the Bird King suggested, "your memories will return."

"My throat is so weak, I can do no more than croak," said the princess.

"That will be fine," said the royal birds, settling themselves into the nest.

Twenty One

The princess croaked, and the lute rang beneath her fingers, its glorious tones filling the nest. She surrendered to the sound, closing her eyes and swaying to the music for hours. When she opened her eyes to bright sunlight, the Frog King's poem had returned to her memory. Once again, she croaked the cryptic words:

> *Things are not what they may seem;*
> *A nightmare may become a dream.*
> *What seems cold and made of stone*
> *May change its form by love alone.*

As the final note rang in the air, an enormous

Golden Frog leaped into the nest. "Good morning, Princess." He bowed. "Your singing is extraordinary!"

"Frog King!" she exclaimed. "You are different. Your skin is golden, and you are larger. But it is beyond that. As the trees in this world are more magnificent than any trees I have ever seen, so too are you more magnificent than when we first met."

"I am father to the Frog King you met earlier," said the Golden Frog, "as the trees here are fathers and mothers to the trees you encountered in your first world."

"My first world," repeated the princess. "Have I died? Is this death? It is nothing like what I have been told."

"No," replied the Golden Frog. "You are more alive now than ever. Here is where you claim your treasure."

"My treasure?" The princess wondered at this word.

"Yes," said the Golden Frog. "The gift you will bring back to your first world."

"And will this gift save my prince?"

"And much more than one man's life," said the Golden Frog. "Did my son's poem provide the answer to the wizard's final riddle?"

Twenty One

The princess closed her eyes and considered. "No, but I feel I am closer to knowing."

"What do you recall beyond the poem?" asked the Golden Frog.

"Your son gave me a gift," she replied, "an emerald, which one day melted in my hand."

"It did indeed," said the Golden Frog. "It changed its form."

The princess smiled then, and her heart opened further. "My love for the prince transformed the precious stone?"

"Yes," said the Golden Frog.

"But how does that answer the wizard's riddle?"

"How indeed?" said the Golden Frog. "I can say only this: *What other impenetrable things might you melt with your love?* Another riddle! Good luck to you. Fear not! Anyone who has come this far will surely make the leap."

His massive hind legs twitched, and he was gone.

For many hours the princess considered the Golden Frog's riddle. As the sky darkened, she fell asleep and dreamed of the fateful day she stood before her parents' court. But now she was an invisible spectator watching a different princess's debut. This princess opened her mouth to sing. She tried, failed, tried again, all while the court and the princes who had come to hear her voice waited in suspense. After a third attempt, this princess smiled brightly into the crowd and declared, "I am either not ready for marriage or my true husband has not yet arrived. I believe that what has occurred today is right and proper. In any case, since we are gathered here, let us celebrate!"

All applauded the princess's wisdom and faith, and the grand banquet did not go to waste. The princess introduced herself to her guests, all of whom admired her beauty and grace. One prince in particular bowed before her, then dropped to one knee. "Will you marry me?" he asked.

"What is this?" cried the king and queen together.

The youngest princess looked puzzled. "How have you chosen me, without having heard my voice?"

"But I have heard your voice," he said gravely. "When you spoke, I heard wisdom and faith—a most beautiful music. If you will have me, I am yours."

The princess saw her future in his eyes and accepted on the spot. All in the kingdom rejoiced.

As the crowd burst into cheers, the princess in

the golden nest awoke, tears streaming down her face. "Such pain my dream has caused me!" she cried. "Why did I have no faith in myself or trust in the world, as did this wiser princess?"

She lay back upon her feather bed and cradled the lute, surrendering once again to its sound. As the mysterious music entered her, it illuminated her body, and she could see inside of herself, as if she were made of glass. There, beneath the crown of her head, her brain shimmered, white and hard like a diamond. She rose with a cry, "My thoughts have been my enemies! My beliefs that I am flawed and undeserving of happiness have been as impenetrable as stone! How unloving I have been to myself!"

With these words, the diamond in her head melted into a shimmering pool, and the faith and trust she had known as a child returned and flowed throughout her body.

"Such an idea this is!" the princess cried. "To love oneself despite one's imperfections!"

The Bird Queen glided to her side. "You are almost ready now. You have answered the Golden Frog's riddle and melted your unforgiving thoughts.

Now you are closer to answering the wizard's riddle as well."

The princess's eyes grew brighter. "I see more clearly now."

"You have a new idea now," said the Bird Queen. "For good or for ill, there is nothing more powerful than a new idea."

Twenty Two

She awoke the next day a new princess, for a new idea remakes one—body and soul. She walked around her enormous nest, brimming with gratitude for what she had received and with love for herself, for the prince, and for the world in which she lived and breathed. Hope filled her. As the day grew dark, she lay back upon her feathered bed, cradling her lute. The moon cast a gentle light into the nest as she struck the strings and hissed:

> *Things are not what they may seem;*
> *A nightmare may become a dream.*
> *Within is fruit, without is rind;*
> *Who seems fearsome may be kind.*

As if drawn by these incantatory words, a massive snake twisted over the edge of the golden nest. If the princess felt fear, she did not show it.

"I am mother to the snake you met in your first world many months ago," she hissed. "You have learned our song well. What else do you recall of your meeting with my daughter?"

The princess touched her bare throat. "She gave me her skin, which I wore around my neck. When the wizard tried to strangle me, it burned his hands and saved my life. Later, when I rubbed the skin, the answer to his second riddle was revealed. For that I am grateful."

"Did my daughter's gift provide more than your safety and a riddle's answer?"

The princess stroked the lute and hissed. After a while, she replied, "I recall something even more miraculous. Her skin left a powder on my fingers, and when I touched the wizard's wounded hands, they began to heal in front of my eyes!"

At these words, the snake shrugged off her dark, crackling skin and slithered forth a silvery creature so bright the princess had to cover her eyes.

"Yes!" the princess cried. "Like that! New hands were beneath the wounded ones."

Twenty Two

"Often new life lies beneath a wound," uttered the Silver Snake.

The princess hissed and struck the lute. Once again she imagined the wizard's shabby, wrinkled cloak peeling away and falling to the ground, followed by his old, wrinkled skin. Beneath it all stood a boy clutching a monkey doll. When first she had this vision, she had been searching only for the wizard's childhood treasure. Now she examined the child himself. His eyes were trusting and filled with love. She gasped. Was something beautiful hiding beneath the wizard's ugly exterior? Could she have been so deceived?

"I cannot wrap my mind around this mystery!" she cried. "Is this child the fruit within the rind? The new life beneath the wound? Is the wizard a good man held prisoner by evil, just as I was held prisoner by my loveless thoughts?"

"Some mysteries cannot be solved," responded the Silver Snake, "only accepted—as the sun and moon are accepted—and woven into the tapestry of life."

She began to hiss a soothing silver song.

The princess drifted on the bed of song and moonlight, the answer to the wizard's final riddle awakening within her even as she slept.

Twenty Three

The princess spent the next day wandering her golden bowl, marveling that the evil wizard had once been an innocent child. As she drowsed in the twilight, she began to pluck at the lute and howl a mournful tune. Within moments, a Golden Wolf leaped into the nest and settled beside her, adding his voice to her song.

After a long while he said, "Can you recall the words my son spoke before you parted?"

With a final pluck of the lute, the princess replied:

> *Things are not what they may seem;*
> *A nightmare may become a dream.*

Night is Day and Slow is Swift;
What seems a curse may be a gift.

At her words, the wolf unleashed a mighty howl and opened his eyes wide. Within them, the princess saw first an image of herself crying in her royal bed and rubbing her throat, followed by an image of the beautiful prince looking at her with such love it took her breath away.

"Do you understand these words now?" asked the Golden Wolf.

"I understand now," said the princess, "that the world is not what it may seem and that people are not what they may seem. What seems as hard as stone may be as yielding as water; what seems hideous on the outside may be beautiful within; and what seems to be terrible misfortune may actually be a blessing. Had I received the gift I believed I had been denied at age sixteen, I would never have met my true love. My singing curse was a gift."

"Well stated," said the Golden Wolf. "And do you know the answer to the wizard's final riddle now? Can you apply what you have learned to him as well?"

Twenty Three

Awareness filled the princess's heart. "I can," said she.

"Why then," asked the Golden Wolf, "does the wizard take such pleasure in doing evil?"

The princess sang out, "He does *not* take pleasure in doing evil! That is the answer. He, too, is not what he appears to be. He has been enchanted. Like me, his life took detours he neither wanted nor understood."

"You are no longer blind!" the Golden Wolf exclaimed. "With your hard-earned wisdom, you have answered all of the wizard's riddles, causing the spark of good remaining within him to flare again. It will soon grow to a mighty fire in his soul. By returning him to himself, you have also freed the prince, who waits impatiently for your return."

The princess was overwhelmed. "I have wrought such a miracle?"

The Golden Wolf replied, "Time spent considering another's suffering is often well-rewarded."

"But what of the evil the wizard has wrought?" she asked. "What of the ninety-nine murders? What of the tortures to which he subjected my prince? What of the other unspeakable crimes he has committed?" The princess shuddered.

"That is not your concern," said the Golden Wolf. "Yours is not to judge another's wickedness but to see what good remains."

"But is it not a dangerous practice to search for good in those who appear irredeemable?" she asked.

"Make no mistake, dear princess. Some have progressed too far along the path of darkness to be healed by human compassion. Their spark of love has died, and none can bring it back to life. Their reconciliation will be elsewhere. Trust yourself to know when human love has failed."

The princess took a deep breath and felt her own wisdom and strength. "Thank you for your teachings, Golden Wolf. When I began this journey, I thought only of myself and my desires. I believed I had been unfairly treated, but I did not know of the suffering of others. Nor did I understand that I had within me the power to transform another's life."

"You are welcome, good princess." The Golden Wolf disappeared.

"Royal birds!" the princess called into the sky. "My fledgling days have ended. I am ready to leave the nest!"

Twenty Three

No sooner had she spoken, than they appeared.

"Climb upon my back, Princess," said the Bird Queen. "We will return you to your first world."

Twenty Four

When next the princess woke she found herself floating in a pond beneath a sky full of stars. The redolence of nearby flowers and the muted sounds of the forest at night soothed her. When had she last luxuriated in a warm bath such as this? Perhaps in the palace of her birth. She smiled at the memory. Had that really been her experience at one time? Bathed by servants? What an unexpected course her life had taken.

All seemed dreamlike now as she lay in the water—awake but not awake, asleep but not asleep. That is a strange land, as anyone will tell you. The world is here but also there, and in that world, a

woman's rich, clear voice began to sing. The words
seemed familiar to the princess:

All are perfect; none are wrong.
Trust in me and in this song.
People grow in different ways.
Flowers bloom on different days.

All are perfect; none are wrong.
Nothing sad will last for long.
Some say life is but a dream;
Things are not what they may seem.

All are perfect; none are wrong.
Never fear you don't belong.
Time is young and time is old.
Trust the myst'ries to unfold.

The princess found herself singing along, amazed
that she knew the words. And as she sang, tears spilled
from her eyes and filled the pond. Gentle hands began
to bathe her. Her body rocked in the soothing water.
Her soul rocked in the lullaby's embrace.

Twenty Four

"Who bathes me?" she called into the starry night. "I feel your presence but see no one."

The voice stopped singing and spoke, "Did you learn nothing from the blind Wolf King? Must I be seen to be perceived?"

The princess was silent.

"I will prepare you for your wedding."

"My wedding?" echoed the princess in wonder. "It is finally time?"

"Yes," the voice continued. "Your courage and love were strong enough to free my son. Long years has he been imprisoned in a brutal, loveless world, but you have released him. He will stroll gardens now and not graveyards, and he will do great good in this world."

The princess lay quietly in the water, deep joy suffusing her body and soul. Finally, she spoke, "Through all the painful months I cried in my royal chamber and all the painful months of my journey this question was ever present: *Why did I deserve such sorrow?* Now I ask a new question: *Why do I deserve such joy?*"

The voice responded, "Do you need to know why the sun hangs in the sky to feel its warmth?"

The princess considered these words.

The voice continued, "Why is one infant welcomed into the world with love and another with cruelty? Why does a kind man die young, while a cruel man live to old age? Some believe it is simply good or bad fortune, mirrored in the stars at the moment of birth; some that debts from previous lives are being paid; and some that struggle is preparation for a great destiny. There is no answer. All must learn to live in the mystery of the universe."

"Wondrous are your words," said the princess. "I feel their truth, yet I cannot keep myself from asking questions."

"It will come with time," said the voice. "Already you have grown so wise."

The princess smiled in the water to hear that she was wise.

"Now you have but one final task," said the voice.

A wave of weariness washed over the princess. "My tasks are not complete?"

"If one is alive, one's tasks are never complete," chided the voice.

The princess was chastened. "I am honored to do my duty."

Twenty Four

"You must return the lute to its rightful owner."

"The lute!" the princess exclaimed, feeling around in the water.

"Do not fear. It lies safe and dry on the bank."

"The Bird King and Bird Queen gave it to me. Let me call to them!"

"They are not the lute's rightful owner. They merely safeguarded it for you."

"Who is its rightful owner?" asked the princess.

"Sleep now," murmured the voice, as gentle hands combed out the princess's hair in the water. "When you awaken, you will be dressed and ready for your wedding. Follow your heart, as you have learned to do so well. You will know to whom the lute belongs.

The princess slept in peace and dreamed of new worlds.

Twenty Five

But what of Zadri and the prince?

As you may recall, Zadri was about to step outside into his gruesome garden of death, where the evil he had wrought would be revealed once and for all. He knew it would be the end of Simian's love for him, but he could not bear to deceive the good creature a moment longer.

With a sinking heart, he pushed open the heavy castle door. Casting his eyes down in shame and grief, he awaited Simian's horrified cries.

"Zadri, it is more beautiful than in my wildest dreams!" sang the delighted monkey. "No wonder you have been unwell, cooped up inside your chambers when you could have been outside in this paradise!"

Unable to believe his ears, Zadri lifted his gaze and was unable to believe his eyes! No dark cemetery spread before him. Instead, he saw a grove of such magnificence his breath was taken away. Where were the graves he had ordered the prince to dig and the headstones he had forced him to build? In their place stood ninety-nine exquisite trees. At the base of each tree stood a lovely young woman, basket in hand, gathering fruits or flowers, whichever bounty the tree produced. The air was fragrant and alive with birdsong. Fawns peeked from behind bushes, rabbits dozed in the grass, squirrels chittered in the branches.

Zadri could barely breathe. He stepped into the sunlight. Simian bounded from tree to tree, greeting the young women.

Had he died? Zadri considered this as he contemplated his surprising surroundings. Who were these beautiful young women? Who had planted these trees? Where was the grim world he had known?

"How much time have we," asked one of the women, "to prepare the banquet and the decorations?"

"The banquet?" Zadri echoed.

"My wedding, good Zadri. Have you forgotten?"

Twenty Five

Zadri turned to see the prince he had tortured for so many years smiling at him. His radiant face and strong body showed no signs of ill health. He was garbed in a royal robe. At his side stood his father, the king whom Zadri had murdered and whose body he had cast into the dungeon. He, too, was handsome and hale, garbed in a fine cloak.

Now Zadri was certain he had died. Or perhaps he was dreaming or had lost his mind. Why did the prince and his father look at him with such kindness?

"Mother!" cried the young man. "Zadri has forgotten what today is!" In the distance, Zadri saw the queen whose happiness he had destroyed when he killed her husband and kidnapped her son so many years ago. He felt faint and leaned against a tree to steady himself.

The queen drew near, carrying a dark red rose, which she pinned to her son's robe. "Zadri most certainly has not forgotten your wedding day!" She kissed her son on each cheek and then turned to embrace the wizard, whispering. "Fear not. The compassion of others has healed you. You have been reborn."

"But—but—how?" Zadri stammered. "Why?"

The queen took his arm and walked him away

from the crowd of wedding guests. "*How* and *Why* are not the right questions," said she. "*Where* is more to the point."

"Where?" Zadri murmured.

"Yes." The queen smiled a lovely, warm smile that Zadri could barely endure. Guilt overwhelmed him. She continued, "You have been lost for many years—enchanted by a dark master you barely remember. He lured you with the promise of magical knowledge and then led you far from your heart into a love-less world. His vile spell caused you to perpetrate evil deeds, which could never satisfy you, no matter how often you professed your pleasure in commit-ting them. When Simian was brought to life, you returned to the innocent palace of your childhood heart. In this place—in this "where"—all you truly want to do and to be has been restored to you. Ask no more questions. Rejoice at the goodness of a bene-factor who has released you from your prison."

"I was in prison?" whispered Zadri. "I thought I was free. Unhappy but free."

"Those two words can never go together," said the queen.

"I am so confused," whispered Zadri. "Long-ago

memories are returning. Of a cruel father who beat me and had no love for me. I closed my heart to protect myself. How will I be safe now?"

"Your safety was an illusion," said the queen. "When you closed your heart to the pain you had endured, you became half a man. You have been incomplete, Zadri, and have labored through your life, guided only by your mind. Without your heart to inform you, you have lacked wisdom. That is why you could not recognize evil when you met your master, and why you were so easily enchanted. You were not safe at all!"

"I wanted to be free from unhappiness," Zadri said woefully. "That is the other reason I closed my heart."

The queen regarded him. "Were you happy in your evil?"

"No!" Zadri cried. "I was never happy as an evil wizard."

"That is all that you need to understand. You are free to live now, happy and complete."

"But how can I accept such a gift?" Zadri was miserable. "I who have caused such pain to others? I have been worse than the cruel father who raised me."

"Accept it you must," declared the queen. "What you have wrought has been unwrought. Who was dead has been returned to life. All memories have been wiped clean. To the princess alone do you owe an apology. She will soon arrive."

"May I make no reparations for my misdeeds?" Zadri could not yet accept this wondrous thing.

"If others forgive you, you must forgive yourself. You must vow to live within the palace of your heart and to act always and only from love."

Zadri stared around him at the happy people and animals, at the gorgeous trees swaying in the fragrant grove. "If this is living within my heart, why should I want to live otherwise?" he whispered, choked with emotion. He trembled, though, at the thought of the princess and feared her judgment.

Twenty Six

The princess awoke on the grassy bank, dressed in a luminous gown lovelier than any she had ever seen. Freshly plucked flowers adorned the hem, and petals of various shapes, sizes, and colors were woven into the fabric itself. On her head rested a grass wreath studded with dark red roses. The lute lay beside her. At her feet were a frog, a snake, and a wolf. A bird perched in a nearby tree. "Princess, you are a radiant bride!" the animals chorused. "Let us guide you to your wedding!"

"Long have I dreamed of this day!" she cried, rising and hanging the lute over her shoulder. She followed her escorts into a sunny clearing and then onto a path leading through a grove. Streamers of all the colors of the rainbow waved on the branches, and laughter rang in the distance. Beyond the grove towered a palace.

Suddenly a small monkey dressed as a wizard bounced into her arms. The princess laughed and lifted him to her face. "Hello, little friend! What is your name? I believe I have seen you before in a dream."

"My name is Simian," said the monkey. "Zadri, my best friend in the world, brought me to life." The creature gazed into her eyes. "You are so beautiful! Are you the princess we have been waiting for? Your eyes sparkle and dance like a princess, and you speak with a regal voice."

"Thank you for your kind words," she said.

"Yes. I am certain you are the princess of whom Zadri speaks so highly. Hurry! We cannot begin without you!"

He jumped to the ground and pulled at her skirt to hasten her.

She moved with a weightless joy toward the huge pavilion set up before the palace. The longing to be united with her prince was so great she could barely breathe.

Twenty Six

All at once she froze. The wizard—was it he?—came toward her, carrying a shimmering crown of diamonds and multi-colored gems. He looked like the wizard, and yet he did not. For one thing, this man was younger and had kind eyes. He stopped a foot away from her and bowed.

"Zadri!" shouted Simian. "I have found the princess. See how beautiful she is. Hurry, Zadri! I have always wanted to attend a wedding!" Simian chattered in a frenzy of excitement. He did not notice the apprehension that crossed the wizard's face as the princess studied him.

Zadri stood in awkward silence, waiting for the princess to expose him for who he was. The forgiveness he had been offered by the prince and his family would mean nothing if the princess told her tale. Simian would at last know what an evil person he had been. Two tears, one silver and one gold, trembled in the corners of his eyes.

The princess saw these tears. A shock of recognition, of sympathy and love, shuddered through her body. "Zadri!" she cried, taking his hand. "How wonderful to see you again. I did not recognize you, but it is only because you have grown more handsome! Simian, is this the friend of whom you spoke? He is a wonderful wizard. You are very lucky to have him for your friend."

Simian bounced to Zadri's shoulder, hugged him, and then scampered off through the trees, drawn by the sounds of merrymaking.

Now Zadri's tears flowed freely, tears of gratitude, shame, and happiness. He placed the crown above the wreath of flowers on the princess's head and whispered, "Thank you. You are a true princess. Your grace astounds me. I beg your forgiveness of all that I forced you to endure. A dark master held me in thrall, and only now have I been freed."

The princess nodded. "I, too, was held captive in a prison of my own making. Time and again I was offered help by a singing man and by many wise animals who tried to disenchant me, but I clung to my false beliefs. Only in another world did I break the spell. I was ashamed to learn that I had enchanted myself with my unloving thoughts."

Zadri flinched. "I must still battle such thoughts. They are indeed dark masters. I do not understand why we so easily fall under their spell."

"Nor do I," responded the princess, "but I am

learning that I do not need to understand every-thing. Understanding does not make one happier or more loving."

Zadri nodded. "You are wise."

She smiled. "Much of my life now seems like a dream, but it is all behind me. I have only the present and the future to tend to."

At this moment, the queen approached and extended a hand to her future daughter-in-law. "Brave and loving daughter, thank you for every-thing you have endured for the sake of my son. You have restored our family, and with gratitude and joy we welcome you into our lives."

The princess smiled and bowed.

Zadri clapped his hands. "The wedding! Let us begin!"

He took the princess's right hand, and the queen took her left, and they walked her to the pavilion where the prince and the king waited.

Then Zadri, Simian, the young women, and the animals formed a circle around the royal family.

The prince walked toward her, a crown of silver and gold gracing his head. He bowed deeply. "Dear Princess," he spoke. "I loved you at first sight, for

I saw your beauty and courage as you spoke fearlessly to the heartless wizard. His evil was no match for your kindness and wisdom, and he has been destroyed to the benefit of all."

Zadri gave an uncomfortable cough.

The prince continued. "Good Zadri has taken his place, and with his magic he has restored peace, beauty, and order to our world."

Simian felt as though his heart would burst with pride. Such determination and energy it must have taken to battle the evil wizard. No wonder Zadri had been ill.

The prince knelt and raised his eyes. "If you will have me, my love, Zadri will marry us here and now."

The king and queen gazed with pride upon their son.

The princess's heart was so full she could barely speak. "Dear Prince," she began, "I loved you at first sight, for I saw your beauty and your compassionate heart. Even in the depths of your grief and pain, tortured as you were by the evil wizard, you valued my welfare above yours. I want no man more than you."

As she bent to take his hand, the lute she had forgotten she was carrying slipped from her shoulder.

Twenty Six

"Oh!" she cried. "I must return this lute to its rightful owner before we can marry. Your mother told me last night as she bathed me in the pond and dressed me for my wedding."

The queen looked confused. "What is this lute of which you speak? What is this pond? Daughter, I did not bathe you last night."

Twenty Seven

The princess stared in surprise at her future mother-in-law. "You did not bathe me? Nor thank me for saving your son? You did not tell me of my final task?"

"I know nothing of this, dear princess," said the queen.

The princess gazed at the lute. "It seems I have been presented with a mystery."

She stood quietly, reflecting upon the lessons of her long journey. Then she smiled, adjusted the lute's strap around her neck, and began to pluck the strings and to sing the words she now knew by heart.

All are perfect; none are wrong.
Trust in me and in this song.
People grow in different ways.
Flowers bloom on different days.

All are perfect; none are wrong.
Nothing sad will last for long.
Some say life is but a dream;
Things are not what they may seem.

All are perfect; none are wrong.
Never fear you don't belong.
Time is young and time is old.
Trust the myst'ries to unfold.

All were stunned at her exotic voices as she croaked, hissed, howled, and shrieked. The prince found all of them magnificent and fell even deeper in love.

As the lute's final note hovered in the air, a woman appeared before the princess. "I am she who bathed you last night."

At the sound of her voice, Zadri gave a great start.

The woman turned to Zadri and laid her right

Twenty Seven

hand upon his cheek with great tenderness. Her left she placed upon his right shoulder. "My son, I was denied the joy of welcoming you into the world when you were born. I welcome you now." She embraced him.

"M—Mother?" Zadri stammered, pulling away. "You died when I was born. Father told me repeatedly that I had been responsible for your death. And yet your voice is familiar."

"I spoke and sang to you for months while you were in my womb. Of course, you know my voice. Nor were you responsible for my death. No innocent babe can be held accountable for the sorrows that attend his birth."

"But how are you now alive?"

"How indeed?" she said with a smile, turning toward the princess. "Brave and loving princess, there is a story you must hear. In his innocence and with a heart broken by his father, my son met an evil sorcerer who made false promises and enchanted him, prophesying: *You shall do my bidding until the day a maiden who can sing to the four levels of the world—from the frog to the snake to the wolf to the bird—shall set you free.* This dark master forced Zadri to do his wicked will for many years. But you released him. The enchantment is now but dust."

Confused, the princess said, "Zadri was the man I was meant to save? Not the prince?"

"Finding your true love was but a happy accident, which can frequently occur when one follows one's path," responded Zadri's mother.

"I can barely breathe," said the overwhelmed princess.

"Yes," Zadri's mother said. "When one's purpose is finally revealed, it can take one's breath away."

The princess, filled with wonder, looked at her prince and then at Zadri. "How complicated and amazing life is!" she cried. "I followed my path correctly, even though I did not know my true destination."

"Mysteries often take a lifetime to unfold," Zadri's mother continued. "Had you not arrived when you did, and had you not solved the riddles, the heartless sorcerer would have destroyed this kingdom, the entire countryside, people and animals, flowers and trees. Your courage, determination, wisdom, and compassion saved more than just my son! A country owes its freedom to you!"

Twenty Seven

At these words, scores of people, young and old, came streaming into the grove, bearing wedding gifts and cheering for the princess and the prince—and for Zadri, who couldn't take his eyes off his mother's face.

"You must share your story far and wide," she continued. "That will be your life's task. The world is filled with sorrow because people do not understand the great story of which they are a part. They mistake the tiny chapter of their own lives for the entire book and do not recognize that they are also a part of others' stories."

"May I remember this for the remainder of my life!" cried the princess. Then she turned to address the crowd. "I am blessed to have been a part of all of your stories."

"All spells are broken, all enchantments shattered," Zadri's mother spoke. "When a stranger offers compassion to one who does not seem to deserve it, the world begins anew for all involved."

All present bowed their heads at these words.

"Now, Princess," she spoke. "Please give the lute to its rightful owner so the wedding can begin."

The princess turned in a slow circle, placing her

right hand on her heart, as she regarded the prince, the queen, the king, the young women, Zadri and his mother, Simian, and all who had come from the surrounding countryside to celebrate her wedding. She considered each person. Not one face, regardless of the smile it wore for the occasion, was without a trace of grief, pain, anger, or fear.

Once again she addressed the crowd. "The lute belongs to all of us. It is meant to be passed and passed again, for we all need to be reminded of the truth within our hearts—that we are part of a great story even now being written, and that few are beyond forgiveness." She lifted the lute from around her neck and offered it to the first person within reach.

And that is the end of this tale. If you were led to believe that it was only a love story about one princess and one prince, and if you are sorry not to hear more about their wedding and their happy life beyond it, you can hardly be blamed. You were only given one chapter at a time, just as you are given in your own life, and you cannot know the meaning of a story until you have read the entire book.

The Yellow Bird

One sunny day a little boy was playing by himself in the woods. As he walked along, stopping here and there to pat a friendly squirrel or blow the top off a dandelion, he suddenly remembered that the next day was his mother's birthday.

At that very moment something caught his eye. A beautiful yellow rose, the color of the sun, shone from within a patch of otherwise ordinary yellow roses. Compared to the other blooms, it was a little bigger, a little more perfect, and a little more yellow.

"There is my dear mother's gift," thought the boy with satisfaction, and he strode to the rose patch, picturing how lovely the yellow rose would look in a glass jar on the kitchen table.

But as he reached for the rose, it suddenly opened and stared at him. The rose was not a rose but a small yellow bird sleeping with his head tucked under his wing! The boy stared in wonder as the yellow bird cocked his feathered head and stared at him sleepily.

"Good day to you," the yellow bird said, yawning a very small yawn. "I suppose it must be time." He fluttered his wings and stretched his tiny legs, one at a time, then blinked his eyes rapidly and gave himself a shake. "Well, let's be off then!" he said to the boy and soared into the air.

"Wait!" said the boy as he ran after the bird. "What do you mean 'it's time?' Time for what? Where are we going?"

"Time for this and time for that," twittered the bird merrily. "Oh, it feels grand to fly again, I must

The Yellow Bird

say! I've been asleep for a very long time." And the yellow bird darted into the distance.

The little boy followed without a moment's hesitation. Forgotten was his mother's birthday. Adventure was upon him, and he knew he would follow the yellow bird to the end of the world, if he must, because he was just that kind of a boy and the yellow bird was just that kind of a bird. You would do the same thing, I'm sure.

The little boy chased the yellow bird for hours and days and miles and miles. When he grew weary, he sometimes had the sensation that he was no longer running but was, in fact, riding on the yellow bird's back, being borne above strange and fantastic landscapes and worlds of which he had only dreamed. When his weariness left him, he would catch sight of the yellow bird in the distance and realize he couldn't possibly have been riding on his back. Why, the yellow bird was scarcely bigger than his hand!

At times the thrill of his own wild energy would fill him with a greater joy than he had ever known. It was as if the more he ran, the stronger and more energetic he became, until one bright and windy day he sensed that he had ceased to run and had begun to fly instead. His arms, instead of pumping close to his sides, began to stretch out wide away from his body, and he no longer felt his legs or feet.

A few days later, while drinking from a clear pond, he saw, shining in the water, not the human face he had once worn, but a sharp yellow face with bright black eyes like seeds, and wings for arms. He and the yellow bird had become one.

One day he saw in the distance a solitary tree with a simple nest. He felt his heart leap within his breast. "Surely this must be my nest and my home," thought the boy who had become a bird, and he made for it with speed and certainty. As he prepared to enter the nest, however, he saw coiled at the base of the tree a small brownish-gray snake with friendly inquisitive eyes.

"Greetings, yellow bird," said the friendly snake. "I have been preparing for your visit for many years. In all that time, I have perfected my soul, to be worthy of you. I hope you will find this home pleasing, for I know you are to rest here for a while. The wind told me as much, as well as that I am to give myself to you to be eaten for a greater cause."

The Yellow Bird

"Oh, must I eat you?" said the yellow bird anxiously. "You are so kind and dear a snake. Besides I am not hungry and have not been hungry for many days or even years." Yet even as he spoke, the yellow bird was possessed by an all-consuming hunger, as if all the hunger of the previous days and years had been stored up for this moment.

"It is right," said the yellow bird huskily. "I am very hungry and must eat you, but see first that you step out of your skin, for I will need to carry that with me."

So the little brownish-gray snake rubbed herself against a sharp rock and stepped out of her skin. It peeled down easily, revealing the most exquisite yellow snake the yellow bird had ever seen. The snake sparkled and shimmered and sent forth a sunny radiance.

"It is my pleasure and my purpose to become one with you," said the shining yellow snake. "May we together accomplish miracles." And she closed her eyes and awaited her death and new life.

The yellow bird swallowed the snake whole and felt at once a renewal of his strength and an even sharper sense of his own destiny. He slept that night, for the first time in years, in the plain nest of twigs at the top of the tree, wrapped inside the dull snakeskin. When he awoke, his sparkling, shimmering feathers illuminated the world around him for miles.

Away he flew toward an unknown destination, carrying the snakeskin in his beak, never stopping, nor tiring, nor looking in other directions. Though he knew not what his purpose was, nor where he was going, still he flew.

One day after many thousands of miles the yellow bird saw a great castle beckoning in the distance. Richly-hued purple and gold pennants emblazoned with the king's crest fluttered and danced in the breeze. As the yellow bird flew to the branch of a nearby tree, the king's herald was just blowing his horn and preparing to make an announcement. Tucking his snakeskin into a safe nook in the tree, the yellow bird cocked his head and listened very intently, his black seed eyes fixed upon the herald.

"The king wishes it to be known," bellowed the herald, "that he will give half his kingdom and eternal friendship to whomever can answer this question: WHAT IS THE PURPOSE OF LIFE?"

The Yellow Bird

The herald paused dramatically, then repeated, "WHAT IS THE PURPOSE OF LIFE?" He gazed imperiously into the crowd. "It goes without saying that heads will roll if anyone dare waste the king's time on foolishness. Don't bother coming to the palace and requesting an audience with the king unless you are *sure* you know the Purpose of Life, for he hasn't time to waste on idle speculation." The herald disappeared into the palace.

At once the crowd flew into a frenzy of conversation.

"How intelligent is our king!" cried one.

"How grand a question!" whispered another.

"Fancy even thinking up a question like that!" chortled another, scratching his head and looking very confused.

Many more forgot the question at once, because it made them very uncomfortable. One man jumped upon his horse and left the kingdom forever, saying, "If a man can't be free to live without such troublesome questions hanging over his head, then I no longer wish to live here!"

The only quiet being in the whole kingdom was the yellow bird. Perched safely inside the nook of the tree in front of the king's castle, he slept happily and easily, wrapped in his snake skin. He would need much rest, for tomorrow, he knew, would be a very big day.

At the first hint of dawn, the yellow bird opened his eyes and stretched. Then he flew to the king's sleeping chambers and rested on the windowsill, gazing into the room. The king's guard stood straight and watchful at the end of the royal bed. The yellow bird began to twitter a strange and lonely song, and within minutes, the guard was sound asleep. Then the yellow bird hopped to the pillow upon which lay the head of the king.

The king was a wise and noble man. He had ruled his people as well as he knew for a long time, even after the death of his wife three years before from a strange malady that had mystified the court physicians, and even after his beloved young son had fallen to the same strange illness. He had not taken another wife, though his loneliness sometimes made him cry out in the night, and his face wore a perpetual shadow of grief, though he tried his best to hide it.

All this and more the yellow bird perceived just by staring at his face. There was a kindness and

The Yellow Bird

a gentleness to his features that the yellow bird responded to at once, and his bird-heart filled with intense love and empathy for the king and a desire to remove the sorrow and darkness from his features. Just then the king opened his eyes and saw the yellow bird looking at him.

"Greetings, tiny subject!" exclaimed the king. "How is it that you have come to waken me this morning? To what do I owe this great honor?" And the king smiled at the yellow bird, his eyes twinkling, though the yellow bird could see the grief beyond the twinkle, like a lonely fish at the bottom of a pool.

The yellow bird's heart filled with even more love as the king smiled at him. He felt he had never loved a human being quite so much in his life except for his own dear human mother, now thousands of miles and as many years away. He stared with love at the king, his black seed eyes luminous, and said, "I have come to help you discover the Purpose of Life."

Up until he had said the words, the yellow bird had no idea this was his true mission in life, yet as soon as they were uttered, he realized their truth: Here was the reason he had flown so long and so hard for so many years.

The king sat up in bed and rubbed his temples. His first impulse was to laugh at the idea of a tiny yellow bird helping him, a great king, discover the Purpose of Life. Yet, as I mentioned earlier, he was a wise king and a good man and knew better than to turn away from anyone, no matter how small, who might offer to show him the way.

"Tell me, wise little bird," the king said judiciously, "what is the Purpose of Life? I have grown old and weary from the question running always through my head, and from the meaninglessness I feel in my own life and sense in the lives of others. Are we put here in this world for a reason? Or do we just spring up like so many blades of grass, haphazardly and with no detectable pattern? Does death bear fruit? Does anyone greater than myself know or care that my wife and child have died? Or that only yesterday I removed their dark flags from the parapets? Tell me, what is the Purpose of Life?" Even as he spoke the king began to feel a growing sense of comfort, though he did not know it was the due to the nearness of the yellow bird.

The yellow bird said then, "Dear King, I will do better than tell you the Purpose of Life. I will help you discover it for yourself. Surely it could not be that only a few should know the answer to something so important. It must be that each of us is able to discern his or her own Purpose, if only given a little help. I do not know your purpose, but I might help you discover it. You did not know my Purpose, and yet you *are* my Purpose." And the yellow bird hopped to the king's chest.

"Stroke me, please," he said to the king, "for I am weary from my long journey and need to be comforted. Please hold me and care for me for a few moments, and then I will help you discover the Purpose of Life."

So the king gently stroked the tiny yellow bird and held him and comforted him after his long journey, and as his fingers brushed against the yellow bird's feathers, memories of his wife and son sprang up in his mind and in his heart. And he noticed, with great surprise, that the memories did not sting so terribly while he was stroking and comforting the yellow bird. Though his wife seemed more beautiful and loving than ever, and his son more handsome and brave, still their nearness in his thoughts did not fill him with the usual heavy grief. In fact, he was even able to enjoy his memories, and he felt nearer to his dead wife and son, and not quite so alone. Tears streamed from his eyes, but they were healing tears, and each one reduced by one drop the pond of sorrow inside his heart. Love for the yellow bird grew and filled him with a joyous yellow light.

"Dear yellow bird!" the good king cried. "Am I discovering now? Is this my Purpose? To love and comfort another during the long journey through life? For as I touch you, I feel Love calling my name after so long. And while Love is calling, I find I do not need another Purpose."

The king continued to stroke the yellow bird. With each touch of the bird's feathers, his expression grew lighter and clearer, and the shadows lifted from his face and dissolved in the morning light.

The yellow bird replied, "Great King, I am but an instrument of revelation. I was sent to help you discover your Purpose, yet I did not know it myself. Only you could know. Still, it seems right to me that your Purpose is to love and comfort others on their journeys. Others may have different purposes. That is not for me to know." The yellow bird trembled a little. "Father King, I grow very tired, as I feel my life is nearing its end. Please, do this thing for me: There is a snakeskin hidden in a nook in the tree outside your castle. When I am dead, pull the snakeskin over my body and place me high in the tree. And may the world watch over us both." And with these words, the yellow bird spoke his last.

The king did as he was instructed, wrapping the tiny body inside the snakeskin and placing it high in the tree. Then he mourned all the day and night in his chambers. "I loved my wife with all of my heart, and she was taken from me," he cried. "And my young son, whom I loved more than my life, was taken also." He wept more. "And now, the tiny yellow bird I have learned to love has been taken from me! Oh, everything was so clear a moment ago, but now with the death of my beloved yellow bird, I find myself mired in shadows again, and try as I might I cannot remember my Purpose."

And the king stared from his window into the tree outside the castle and mourned the tiny yellow bird with all of his heart. Looking down, he saw a wild dog sniffing around the base of the tree and barking. The dog was skin and bone, uncared for, and his fur was matted and tangled. The dog seemed familiar, though he did not know why. Suddenly he remembered with horror that the dog had belonged to his son.

"Oh, miserable dog," he cried, "all the long while I have been mourning my wife and son, you have been mourning too, and I never noticed. We could have been comforting each other on our journeys through grief and despair."

And the king hastened to the tree and gathered up the stray dog in his arms and carried him to his chambers. There, he bathed and brushed him and set him on his royal pillows and fed him. Then he stroked the dog's newly shining fur all the long night as he gazed from his window until he at last fell asleep.

The next day there appeared bright and early at the palace a young boy of extraordinary beauty and bearing. The guards all spoke amongst themselves, "Surely, this must be a king's son! Note his bearing and his eyes!" The young boy asked for an audience with the king and was granted one on the spot.

The king gazed with admiration upon the beautiful boy and thought sadly, "Ah, would that my own dear son had lived. He would have carried himself like this young man."

The Yellow Bird

The king's dog raced about the young man like a puppy, excitedly sniffing and wagging his tail and barking joyous barks.

"Great King," the boy spoke solemnly, "I have come here though I know not why. I was picking a yellow rose for my mother's birthday, and I chased a yellow bird for a while, and this morning I awoke at the foot of yonder tree, finding myself in this strange land." The boy looked deeply into the king's eyes.

The king stared in amazement into the bright black eyes of the yellow bird sparkling in the boy's face, and then he gazed up into the tree in which he had placed the body of the yellow bird.

"He was right," the king whispered half to himself. "I was his Purpose, and he my Revelation."

"Come in, come in!" he welcomed the beautiful youth. "I will help you search the countryside for your father and mother."

"My father is dead," said the boy matter-of-factly. "He died when I was very young, and I never knew him. My mother and I live alone at the edge of the woods."

So the mother was brought to the palace, and, as often happens when magic is afoot, no time had passed at all since her son had gone to the woods that fateful day, so she hadn't even missed him yet.

When the king saw the boy's mother, her beauty and bearing reminded him of his dead wife, and he asked her to marry him on the spot.

There was a wedding the very next day–the mother's birthday–and she said it was certainly the best present she ever could have expected. For her bridal bouquet, the young boy gathered his mother an armful of yellow roses.

And the king and his new wife and new son (and the dog) lived happily ever after, and once a week the king gathered his court and all the townspeople around him and told them the story of the yellow bird and about finding one's Purpose, and about how Love was as good a Purpose as any, if you could discover no other.

And where there once was sorrow now there was joy, for that is the way of most stories if one is only patient enough to hear them through to the end.

The Woodcutter's Daughter

Way at the end of the woods lived a wood-cutter and his daughter. It had just been the two of them for many a long year. If it were not for the soft, white rabbits leaping through the frozen fields, the girl would have never seen a soul but for her unhappy and unkind father.

Day after day, full of rage and misery, the wood-cutter left for the great, dark woods and chopped away from dawn to dusk. At noon, his little daughter raced through the frozen fields to bring him his lunch—a meager dish it was, but it would have to do, for that was all they had.

At dusk, the woodcutter would clump home in a black spirit and slam the door of the cottage, making the little girl jump and quake with fear.

"Where is my dinner?" he would growl.

After the little girl brought him whatever small meal she had made, he would rise from the table in darkness and go to the chair near the fire and snore and grunt and growl in his sleep. The little girl would wake him after a while and help him to his bed.

One night, after kissing him lightly on the cheek, she said, "Papa? I was wondering if you could buy me a little music box the next time you go into town to sell your wood. Just a very small, inexpensive one. . . it would help to pass the long hours while I am alone all day, and I do believe the music would lighten our hearts." And she waited, holding her breath.

"Music box!" her father exploded. "What do we need with a music box? We need food and clothes and shoes—ordinary, sturdy things that will allow us to do more work. Poor people do not need light hearts! Light hearts lead to laziness! I shall beat you if you ever mention a music box again!"

And the girl raced to the spot near the dying embers where she slept, and wept great, gulping sobs, and heard her father still grumbling in the other room. All that night she dreamed of a dark red music box carved in the shape of a heart. When she lifted the lid, all the beautiful sounds of the world emerged—babies gurgling, children laughing, men and women singing, animals dancing, flowers growing—all mixed in with the most wondrous music. When she awoke the next morning, the grayness of her existence made her heart cry out.

As she toasted the bread over the fire for her father's breakfast, she began to sing a strange melody. It was full of pain and grief, but there was joy in it as well. "Papa?" she asked haltingly. "Do you think maybe you could buy a pretty cloth for the table and the windows? It's so very dull and dark in here, I fear I shall die." And she cried a little.

"Child!" the brutish man yelled. "We do not need bits of pretty cloth for the windows and tables. What we need is hardy food and sturdy shoes and strong clothing so that we can work harder. That is why human beings were put on this earth—to work—for the animals do nothing all day but frolic and sleep. What is wrong with you?" The man began to roar and rave. "Leave off your dreaming, child, or you will be sorry! See that today you catch that rabbit I've seen near our house and make some rabbit stew. I'm tired of just vegetables and bread every night. I need some meat! Do not waste your day dreaming, or I will beat you when I return!" He slammed out of the cottage, brandishing his huge ax.

The little girl felt her heart breaking again, as it broke every day. Her father would never understand. She leaned back into the fire-ash and daydreamed of the heart-shaped music box and dancing and having a beautiful dress and tiny slippers and a jeweled necklace. The roughness of her life made her weep.

"Dearest child, why are you crying?" whispered a gentle voice. The girl looked up and saw the mother rabbit who came to visit every day as soon as her father clumped off to the woods. She was as soft and white as a cloud and was very old, having lived for many years in this dark and lonely place.

"Good mother rabbit," the little girl wept, picking up the rabbit and placing it on her lap. "My father does not understand that my spirit is hungry for beauty and that my soul cries out to be fed. Worse, today if I don't make you into rabbit stew, he is going to beat me. I feel today I shall die, for I could no sooner make you into stew than I could turn this hovel into a palace." The girl rubbed her cheek against the rabbit's furry head. "You'd better run far away, my friend," she cried. "For if my father does not eat you for dinner tonight, he will search you out tomorrow and shoot you! Run and hide! And take all of your family with you! Tell them my father is in a rage and may kill them all!" And the little girl wept bitterly. "Now I shall lose my only friend, and I shall die of loneliness–if my father does not kill me first."

"Dear child," the rabbit said gently, "I will give my life to save you. Many times you have fed me when I was starving or let me dream by the fire when winter was too harsh for my old bones. My children are all grown, and my husband is dead. I have lived a long, full life. Listen to what I say and all will be well: cook me in your pot tonight, but take my eyes, my tongue, and my heart and bury them outside this house. Sew my fur into a soft pillow for your head. Make my bones into a fine necklace, which you should never remove, even for your bath." And the old white rabbit gazed at the little girl with her gentle eyes.

"If I must kill you, just so his stomach can be filled, I will hate my father until the end of my days," the little girl said. "No! I will not do it! I will simply leave this house so my father cannot beat me or hurt me anymore! I will live in the woods with the rabbits who love me and care for me. My own human father has never shown me the love you have just now shown me. I will come with you!" The girl hurried about the cottage, taking here and there a scrap of clothing and a loaf of bread.

When she turned around she saw, to her horror and amazement, that the old mother rabbit was laid out, dead, and was neatly skinned, her eyes, tongue, and heart set off to the side and all her bones in a tiny brittle pile.

"Who has killed you? Who has done this!" cried the girl, fingering the soft skin of fur laid to one side.

"You cannot change what was meant to be," whispered a soft voice. "It was written that I should give my life this way. Do not scorn my gift and the blessings that will come from it." The girl looked up and saw the white shadow of a spirit in the snow outside her window.

"I am off to new snowy fields," called the rabbit-spirit as it bounded away. "Use my body and my blood wisely. Perhaps one day we shall meet again."

The girl stared in amazement after the rabbit-spirit, then looked to the piles of rabbit meat and bones. She took the meat and placed it in the pot, then added water and vegetables and salt. The eyes, tongue, and heart she buried outside the window of her father's bedroom.

The rabbit's fur she sewed into a little pillow and placed it near the hearth where she slept.

She cleaned the bones carefully and spent the rest of the afternoon tying them into a strange and magical necklace. The rabbit-bone necklace gave the girl a certain power. When she wore the necklace, she could hear the speech of the human heart, but she did not know that as yet.

When her father clumped home in a black rage she was waiting for him with a large plate of rabbit stew and home-baked bread. "Feed me!" he roared. What she heard was, *"Love me!"* And she flew to his side and kissed him and helped him into his chair.

"Father, smell the rabbit stew! Doesn't it smell marvelous? Are you very happy that I killed the rabbit today and made this for you?"

"Bring me a spoon!" he roared. But what she heard was, *"I am sorry, little daughter, that we are so poor we are forced to eat the only friend you have."* He began to eat the soup. Gradually, as his hunger was appeased, he looked around the room. "What have you got around your neck?" he asked unkindly, pointing with his spoon to the necklace of rabbit bones.

She heard, *"What a lovely necklace, daughter! I wish I had bought it for you myself."*

"Yes, isn't it lovely, father? I know you would have bought it for me if you could have afforded it." And the girl touched the lovely necklace happily.

"Take it off!" he roared. "No daughter of mine will wear a necklace of bones! It's the Devil's work!" And he reached to tear it off her neck.

"Let me wear it," is what the girl heard him say. "Oh, no, father," she said. "The old mother rabbit said it must never leave my neck."

Her father reached for it in fury. A burst of thunder cracked the sky, and a voice was heard.

The Woodcutter's Daughter

"LAY NO HANDS ON THE GIRL, OR IT
WILL BE THE END OF YOUR LIFE!"

The woodcutter jumped aside in fear and
looked with new respect at his daughter. "Someone
is watching over you," he said with astonishment.
"And that is all very well, for I don't have the time to
do it." And he made for his bed.

The girl only heard him say, *"I love you, and I'm
happy that you have found a good friend."* "Oh, father,
I love you, too!" she cried, flying to his side and kissing him on his leathery cheek.

That night she slept on her snow white pillow of
rabbit fur among the ashes and dreamed that where
she had planted the eyes, tongue, and heart of the
rabbit a beautiful tree had grown.

And so it came to pass. When she arose with
the cold dawn and went to wake her father for his
day's work, she was amazed to see that a tree of
incredible light and beauty had grown outside his
window overnight and was casting a warm white
glow into his bedroom. She rushed to the window
and gazed with wonder at the tree. Its branches

and trunk seemed to be made of clouds, so white and yielding they appeared. It was heavily laden with strange fruits, transparent and round as bubbles, which floated near the branches but were not attached to them.

"Father!" she cried. "Wake up! See what has grown overnight outside your window! Have you ever seen anything so beautiful?"

Her father sat up in bed and groggily peered out the window. "From whence has this abominable weed come?" he roared. "What have I done to deserve such as this? An ugly weed growing right outside my window and covered with filthy worms to boot! I'll go at once and chop it down!"

What the girl heard was, "*Oh, daughter, it is as lovely as the morning itself! Let us gather some of the magical fruit for our breakfast!*" And she raced joyously for the door, determined to pluck one of the lovely fruits for her father.

She bowed before the tree and thanked the mother rabbit again for her gift. As she was reaching for one of the strange, clear fruits, she saw her father running up behind her, swinging his huge axe. "Father!" she cried. "What are you doing? Why

are you trying to chop down the beautiful tree?"
And she threw herself in her father's path.

"Move out of the way, daughter!" he roared, "Or
you will die as surely as this tree!"

What she heard was, "*This tree has frightened
me! It must be chopped down!*"

"Oh, no, father!" she cried delightedly. "The tree
is a gift for us from the old mother rabbit whose
eyes, tongue, and heart I buried here yesterday! This
tree will make our life better! You will see!" And she
reached for one of the clear fruits. It broke in her
hand, showering cool healing water all over her wrist
and arm. She raised the fruit skin to her lips and
drank the last few drops of water inside of it.

"Father! Taste the heavenly water!" she cried. "It
is as sweet as milk and honey! Truly!"

But her father raced at the tree, swinging his
axe, bent on destruction. Where he hacked at the
tree, bright green cool water sprayed out, drenching
him from head to foot. Dozens of the fruits burst
and dropped their water upon him. Her father's
eyes opened very wide and a stricken look crossed
his face. "Too late I recall the glory of love!" he cried,
and fell to the ground, dead.

"It is time now for you to go out and offer your love to the world," a quiet voice advised the girl. "Your real work is just beginning. Leave your father beneath this tree, where he will sleep until it is time for him to wake. Take with you a basket of this fruit, and remember, do not remove your necklace for any reason."

The girl listened carefully to the voice, then knelt and kissed her father. "Goodbye, papa," she said sadly. "Would that we could have loved each other more. I'm going away now to offer my love to the world. Goodbye." And the girl gathered up her basket of water-fruit and walked into the woods.

She walked for many miles, deeper and deeper into the woods. The fruit from which she had drunk had filled her so well in so many ways that she did not need to eat, drink, or sleep for many days. On her journey she made friends with all of the animals she encountered, and even the hungry wolves came near to be stroked and caressed by the girl. She fed them all from her basket of water-fruit. And no matter how many fruits she gave away, her basket was always full. She fed men and women, soldiers and travelers, and all she met in the woods. The wolves followed her until she came to a green house made of moss in the very heart of the forest. At its door, they licked her hands, bowed, and returned to the woods.

The girl knocked politely on the door of the little cottage. It was opened at once by a strange old man with hair as white as snow. He wore a cloak of green moss.

"Welcome! Welcome!" he smiled. "I have been waiting for you! You have much to do and no time to waste!" And he led her to an enormous hole, the size of a mountain or more, carved into the earth behind his house. The hole stretched from here to there and all the way down again. She gazed questioningly at the old man.

"Go ahead, my dear," he said, smiling kindly. "You may begin your work."

"I'm afraid I don't understand you," said the girl. "What is my work?"

"Why, to fill the lake, of course," said the old man. "Didn't you know what the fruit was for?"

"No, I didn't," the girl said, feeling rather ashamed. "But where is the lake? I see only a huge hole in the ground."

"You will create the lake when you have filled the huge hole with water," the old man said. "I'll show you how."

And he carefully plucked one of the strange fruits from her basket and tapped it gently at the edge of the huge hole, as you would tap an egg. The fruit opened into two soft shells of water which the man then dumped into the hole. The fruit-skin he laid at his side.

"Do you see, my dear?" he asked gently. "Now it is your turn. You may come back inside when you are done." And he kissed her on her forehead and walked back into his cottage.

The girl stared into the basket of fruit and then into the enormous hole in the earth. How could she fill it, one fruit at a time? In spite of her doubts, however, she set to work with vigor and care. Tap, tap, tap went the fruits against the side of the hole. In went the healing water, out went the fruit-skins, piling up beside her like shimmering jewels. She kept on even as it grew dark.

The Woodcutter's Daughter

It seemed to her after a while that she had always sat at that bank, filling the hole up with water. Days and days and nights and nights passed slowly and evenly and with no change in her tap, tap, tapping, then spilling the fruit's water into the hole. Her previous existence as the woodcutter's daughter faded from her memory, and she came to think of the day she met the strange old man in the green moss cloak as the first day of her life. When she was hungry, she ate of the nourishing fruit. Then she continued with her labor.

One day the water rose high enough that the girl could look into its depths. She bent over and saw an old woman, white with age.

"Hello!" she called in a friendly way, for she was quite lonely, having had no one to talk to for several years. "Can you come out of the water and talk to me?"

The old woman in the water moved her lips at the same time as the girl and stopped talking when the girl stopped. For a moment the girl was puzzled. Then she chanced to look down at her hands. They were gnarled and wrinkled, and the hair falling from her kerchief was snow-white.

"Oh, she is I! I am she! It is myself I see in the lake! I am an old woman now!" She looked to her right and saw a mountain of fruit skins, a mountain as big as the hole had been years and years ago, and she realized she was done with her task. She tried to stand, but had trouble rising, so stiff and old now were her bones.

"What a strange life I have had!" said she wonderingly. "Not for me a husband or a baby to love! My whole life has been spent sitting in front of this lake. What did it all mean?"

Just then the old man in the green moss cloak came out of his house and walked to the old woman. "You have finished your task," he said softly. "Now you may reap the rewards of your labor. Watch." And he pointed to the woods surrounding the immense lake the old woman had created. From all directions came old men and women, gnarled and gray, stooped, some with canes and staffs, some barely able to walk, yet all of them hurrying, hurrying toward the lake as if it were drawing them out of the very woods. Splash. The first old man fell into the lake and sank to the bottom, then an old woman, then another old woman, and on and on. Then scores of younger men and women appeared and moved toward the lake. By the hundreds and thousands people filed in slow motion out of the woods, fell into the lake and sank like stones.

The old woman watched in amazement. What did it all mean? She studied the faces of the countless men and women, some of whom she thought she recognized. One man in particular looked very familiar—a woodcutter, still carrying his axe and walking slowly, blindly toward the lake. The old man in the green moss cloak took the axe from his hand and then allowed him to step into the water.

The old woman looked questioningly at the old man. "What will happen now?" she asked.

The old man motioned toward the lake. "Keep watching," he said.

The old woman watched for several hours—or was it days? Years? Suddenly, she heard a splash. A head surfaced. A baby's head crowing, and then another crying lustily, and then another and another and soon the water was full of splashing, singing babies by the hundreds and by the thousands. They swam toward the old man, crawled out of the lake, then lay in little piles on the bank.

"Welcome! Welcome!" said the old man joyfully. "You are all ready to return into the world and spread your loving message! May you do an even better job this time! Go! Go all of you! With my blessing!"

And the babies, one by one, began to crawl away into the forest, some to the left, some to the right, some to the darker areas, some to the lighter, until finally not a trace of them remained.

The old woman looked in wonder at the old man. "It is more than I could have ever dreamed," she said finally.

"But, wait, my child," said the old man. "Do you not seek more for your own reward? Every task done well and with a loving heart deserves a reward in return." And he reached into the folds of his cloak and held out a dark red box carved in the shape of a heart.

The old woman took the box with trembling hands and examined it on all sides, a long-ago memory tapping at the inside of her brain—a memory of a little girl alone in a cottage with a cruel father, without a mother's comfort, without music to lighten her heart. With tears in her eyes, she looked at the old man, who nodded at her encouragingly. Hardly daring to hope, she lifted the heart-shaped lid.

Music flew from the box like birds, like dragons and butterflies. Music danced like bears and honeybees, howled like wolves and angry winds. Music fell from the box, like heavy stones, and music as light as flowers rose into the air. Music roared like kings and golden lions. Music gurgled out like babies drinking at their mothers' breasts, or rocking on their fathers' laps. All the beautiful music in the world was contained within the box, and it engulfed the old woman in its splendor, until she dropped to her knees, unable to bear the glory of it all.

The music went on for hours—or was it days? Years? And as it swelled and surrounded the old woman, the age began to fall away from her body— the stiffness left her bones, the whiteness left her hair, her wrinkled skin turned soft and smooth. And suddenly in the old woman's place there stood a young, healthy girl on the bank of the lake. Her hand went automatically to her neck around which still curved the strange necklace of rabbit bones. The other hand reached down and lowered the lid of the music box. The beautiful music hung in the air a few moments more, and then there was silence.

"Dear Father," she addressed the old man in the green moss cloak, "happiness such as this could not have been intended for me. I do not deserve such a gift." She ran her fingers over her necklace. "I would not have even met you had it not been for the dear mother rabbit who gave her life for me. Will she receive this much happiness as well?"

The old man smiled, saying, "It is good that you do not forget your friends. Now it is right for you to remove your necklace. Take it off and lay it on the ground beside you."

The girl did as she was bid. Her neck felt very free and light and empty, and she touched her naked skin with a strange feeling not unlike fear.

The old man undid the necklace, scattering the bones into various piles. Then he reached into his cloak, brought out more bones, and added a few to each pile. "Now, my child," he said, when he had arranged the bones to his satisfaction, "drop these bones into the healing lake and let us see what has become of your rabbit friend."

The girl dropped the bones in without hesitation and waited upon the bank for a long long time, finally drifting off to sleep. When she awoke, rising from the lake was a beautiful woman with the kindest, most loving eyes the girl had ever seen. She stepped out of the water, and the old man handed her a green moss cloak.

"Thank you," said the beautiful woman, as she pulled the robe about herself. "I have been waiting to return and offer up my love once again." She turned to the little girl. "Do you not recognize me, dear child?" she asked.

And the little girl looked deeply into the beautiful woman's eyes and saw there the eyes of her old friend, the mother rabbit, who had died to save her life.

"Oh!" cried the little girl! "Oh, wonderful rabbit-woman who saved my life! How may I thank you?"

"Your remembering me is thanks enough. The love you held in your heart has brought me back to human life once more. I shall now be your very own mother, and I will love you as my very own daughter." And she held out her arms to the little girl.

The little girl could not speak for a moment, so great was her joy. She carefully placed the music box on the ground, then fell into her mother's arms and stayed there for a long time, delighting in the unfamiliar feeling of a loving embrace. At last she turned to the old man in the green moss cloak.

"Thank you, Father," she said simply. "I know not what I have done to deserve all of this, but I shall accept this happiness with gratitude and grace."

"Your loving heart has brought you all of these gifts," smiled the old man, "as love given is always repaid. It is the Law of the Universe, and even if one must travel to other worlds to receive it, the love is always repaid."

The little girl stood quietly on the bank absorbing this truth.

"And now you have one final task," said the old man quietly.

"I will do whatever you ask and more," said the girl.

"At the end of this forest," the old man began, "lies a woodcutter sleeping beneath a wondrous tree. He is soon to awaken and wonder where his daughter and wife have gone. Hurry to him, both of you, and be prepared to receive more love than you have ever imagined, for he has traveled to another world in his dreaming, and has freed his heart from the chains of rage and despair. I believe he would love to hear music playing when he awakens." And the old man in the green moss cloak lifted the lid of the little girl's music box and then vanished.

And the heavenly music carried the little girl and her mother to the foot of the long ago tree. There her father lay, sleeping, a peace upon his face she had never seen before. "Wake up, Father," she cried joyously. "Wake up and hear the music!"

The Joyfish

Once upon a time an old fisherman rowed into the wilds of the ocean, further than he had ever gone, for he had caught nothing for weeks and was desperate. "Perhaps it was a good thing," he mused sorrowfully, "that my wife and I were never blessed with the child we so longed for. I am barely able to feed the two of us."

And he cast his hook and line into the ocean, hoping fervently for a bite. Almost at once, there was a powerful tug on his line, and he was nearly pulled from his boat. At the same time, something wild and strong leaped inside of his body. The frail boat pitched and swayed, and the old fisherman hung onto his line for dear life.

Suddenly, like two loving arms stretching over the waters, a shimmering rainbow appeared from one end of the sea to the other. Its radiance dazzled the fisherman, and he fell to his knees, still clutching his line. The rainbow's colors were such as he had never before seen. He tried to think of names for them, but there were no words in his language, and besides, the colors kept changing so he could never quite be certain of them. The sea reflected these bewildering colors, and he gazed in wonder at the bright yellow and the crimson waves lapping at his boat, and the tangerine spray crashing in upon him.

"I have heard other fishermen speak of the holy rainbow and the sacred fish at the end of the world," he spoke as if to a listener, "but I thought them to be only idle imaginings. Now I stand on the threshold of the same rainbow. My world is changing, and I fear I shall never be quite the same."

As he stared, enthralled, into the arc of the strange rainbow, there was a tremendous bubbling and boiling beneath him, the waves began to thrash and chop, and his boat pitched up and down

The Joyfish

violently. He couldn't stop the trembling in his hands and knees nor the wild racing of his heart. "I am going to die," he thought, in a sort of wonder. "Yet I don't feel as afraid as I thought I would."

Suddenly, shooting up like a geyser from the depths of the ocean, an enormous fish broke through the water's surface. The fish was a brilliant yellow—or was it crimson? No, it was blue—or perhaps green? All the unearthly colors of the rainbow formed and reformed on its body, so that never for a moment could the old fisherman detect its actual color. At last it swam near enough for him to see that the fish's skin was composed of mirrored scales and that his hook was caught in its mouth.

"Greetings, old fisherman," said the fish, silvery drops of blood pooling near his mouth. "Blessed are you, for you have caught a Joyfish. I am of an ancient race created by the Sun God Himself. Few mortal eyes have ever seen the likes of me. Should you want to address me, my name is Joy." The Joyfish leaped out of the water, and the rainbow turned its mirror-scales a dark crimson.

The old fisherman listened in wonder, still on bent knees in the center of his boat. "I feel as

195

though my heart would break were I to say your name." He wiped tears from his face. "Please, let me take the hook from your mouth and let you drop back into the sea, for surely I will be struck down for having injured a sacred fish. Also, the fact of your talking troubles me. Though my hunger seems greater than this ocean, I could never eat a talking fish."

The Joyfish stared deep into the soul of the old fisherman. "You do not understand," the Joyfish said. "Everything to me is Joy. If I swim into the jaws of a mighty shark, I feel Joy. If the shark crushes me between its teeth, I feel Joy. If I swim out unharmed, I feel Joy. The silvery blood dripping from my mouth fills me only with Joy. And being caught by you and eaten will fill me with Joy as well. Everything that comes to me I accept with Joy, for such is the nature of a Joyfish."

The Joyfish had swum closer and closer to the fisherman and was now resting at the prow of his boat. It spoke again: "All who eat of my flesh shall recall the Joy placed in them before birth, when they swam inside their mothers, as I am swimming now inside of my Mother, the Ocean."

The Joyfish

The Joyfish paused for a moment, with a questioning look upon his face, as if listening to some secret voice. "Eat of my flesh," he said to the bewildered fisherman. And he laid a fin inside the boat. "Please, bring Joy to both of us and eat of my flesh."

The fisherman began to weep.

The rainbow embraced his boat, like two encompassing arms, as he wept before the Joyfish, whose eyes were now golden fiery orbs due to the shifting dance of the colors.

"Eat," whispered the Joyfish. "You do not need a fire or a pan, for my flesh is such that anyone can eat it at once. It will be the beginning of your Joy and of my Salvation."

The fisherman reached down as if in a trance and cut a piece from the body of the Joyfish and placed it in his mouth. The Joyfish tasted like honey, and the old fisherman savored the taste a long time before he finally swallowed. At once, a wave of deep satisfaction rolled over his body, accompanied by a gentle tugging pressure behind his eyes and in his forehead, and then it was over.

The fisherman blinked and gazed out into the world. Everything was brighter and clearer. The radiance of the sun and the splendor of the rainbow almost took his breath away. His hearing had been sharpened, and his sense of smell returned to him. He took a deep breath and laughed with Joy. His laugh sounded to him more robust than he had remembered, and while he was laughing, he saw that the rough, wrinkled skin of his hands had been replaced by shining new skin and that his old body had become that of a very young man.

"Now listen well," said the Joyfish, "*you* did not catch *me*. It is *I* who caught *you*! I have been searching for you for a long time. Follow me, for there are things of which it is now time for you to know. You were too old before, but now you are just the right age." And the Joyfish slipped beneath the waves, leaving a thin trail of silvery blood behind.

The fisherman stepped from his boat into the welcoming sea. "How strange," he thought, as the water closed over his head, "that I never before visited the undersea world." Then all went black.

When he opened his eyes, he found himself in a dark undersea cavern where incandescent flowers and plants, the likes of which he had never before seen, swayed in the silent and eternal ocean waters. The Joyfish hovered next to him, radiating a powerful tranquility. Countless fish, some gold and some silver, swam back and forth before the fisherman's wondering eyes. The Joyfish waved a fin at the gold and silver fish. "Behold!" he exclaimed to the fisherman. "A dance few mortal eyes have ever seen!"

At the Joyfish's signal, the gold and silver fish began to swim in a circle, each with a long silver or gold thread in its mouth. Each gold fish partnered with a silver fish, and then back and forth, back and forth the couple swam with their threads gripped in their mouths, mingling and dancing with other fish, intermingling with other threads, and thereby weaving an intricate tapestry of gold and silver. Though at times the fisherman guessed the next turn of the dance, just as often he was wrong, and he finally ceased his attempts to anticipate the choreography and began to simply enjoy it.

And as he did so, he felt a parallel dance within his own body, felt his blood dancing in and out of his veins in the same mysterious rhythms and patterns as the gold and silver fish. He was in awe at the very wonder of it. He noticed, too, a strange thing—the fish seemed to lose their color as they danced. The tapestry that they were weaving grew more and more radiant, silver and gold, as the fish themselves grew pale and gray.

Suddenly the first fish couple dropped to the floor of the cavern and lay there, unmoving. Then the next couple, and then the next, until the cavern floor was littered with their bodies. The brilliant gold and silver tapestry drifted peacefully in the water and slowly settled over the bodies of the still fish.

The fisherman turned to see the Joyfish weeping silvery tears onto the cavern floor. "No matter how many times I see it," the Joyfish said, his voice trembling, "I am always rendered speechless with Joy. My Joy is so great that I must weep."

The fisherman wept as well, though he could not have said why.

Then the Joyfish swam to the tapestry and picked it up in his mouth. The bodies of the fish beneath it had vanished. The Joyfish carried it to the fisherman and laid it at his feet. The fisherman saw then that the gold and silver tapestry was, in fact, a long robe, scaled as were the fish with iridescent bits of glinting silver and gold.

"A royal cloak fit for a king," said the Joyfish joyfully, and he beckoned to the fisherman to put on the cloak.

The fisherman shied away from the glistening robe. "Oh, no!" he exclaimed. "I cannot wear such a cloak! I am no king! You have chosen the wrong man."

"Of what are kings made?" asked the Joyfish. "Are they not flesh and blood and bone, as are you? I have chosen you rightly and carefully. Now put on the robe."

The fisherman felt as though he could not disobey the Joyfish. He picked up the robe, which was as light as light itself, and carefully wrapped it around himself.

Meanwhile, in the upper world, the fisherman's wife was kneeling at the edge of the sea, weeping and tearing her hair. Her husband had not returned that day, though his frail boat had miraculously found its way home to the very part of the shore upon which she waited. The poor old woman embraced the boat and cried out, wild with grief, "My dear old husband who has loved me and protected me my whole life has met up with some evil. No doubt, that which I have dreaded for years has finally happened—a whale has swallowed him, or he has been eaten by sharks, or lured into the underwater world by an entrancing siren. Even as I speak, the siren may have stolen his soul and left his poor body to founder in the unwelcoming sea. A wretched life of need we have lived, yet still it was our life, no better or worse than others' lives, save for that we were unable to have a child. Still, we loved each other as well as we knew, though perhaps it was not the best we could have done."

The old woman paused for a moment in her mourning and gazed into the empty boat with sorrow. Tucked away in a corner, she saw a pile of what appeared to be cloth. She pulled it from the boat. The cloth was unlike any she had ever seen or felt. It was as light as a feather, yet seemed as sturdy as rope, and was spun of coarse gray and brown thread. As the old woman felt of the cloth, she looked into the distance and saw a dim rainbow forming over the ocean.

The Joyfish

"This cloth will be my shroud," said she, gazing out at the rainbow. "And as this wooden boat held and rocked my husband all the years of his life, so now in death it shall hold and rock me."

And she stepped with great care into the boat, for her bones were stiff with age, and covered herself with the strange cloth. Amazingly, though it was very chilly and windy on the shore that day, she felt instantly warm and shielded. "Dear husband," she cried, "I was not meant to live alone in this world. But hold onto your soul until I am with you once again!"

She closed her eyes, and as the tide carried away her coffin-bed with a rush and a sigh, she was lulled into a peaceful sleep.

While she slept, the waves carried her to the very same spot her husband had ventured the day before. The rainbow was burning with unearthly colors when the old woman suddenly awoke.

"Where am I?" she whispered in fright and awe, gazing with wild eyes at the rainbow. Vivid tangerine and mint green waves danced and leaped around her boat, sparkling and changing colors with the rainbow. The old woman stared at the water in amazement and then back at the rainbow. She then looked down and saw that the coarse gray and brown cloth she had covered herself with had become a robe of dazzling silver and gold.

"It really *is* a shroud," the old woman said in wonder. "Though it is of a finer quality than I could ever have afforded. What is the meaning of this? Where am I, and who has wrapped this royal robe around me?"

At that very moment, a dolphin broke through the ocean's surface, its gleaming skin a palette of the rainbow's changing colors. It bobbed in the water and looked curiously at the old woman who almost fainted with fright. The dolphin slapped the water furiously with its flippers, sending a crashing spray into the old woman's coffin-bed.

"Please! Please, don't eat me!" the old woman cried, staring with horror into the dolphin's shining black eyes which seemed to grow larger and deeper the longer she stared.

"I don't want to eat you," said the dolphin in a strange high voice. "I am a messenger. Climb onto my back, and I will carry you to the next stage of your journey."

The Joyfish

Then the dolphin leaned into the boat, causing the old woman to shake with terror, and dropped a ring into the old woman's lap. "Is that not your wedding ring?" the dolphin asked in a friendly manner.

The old woman stopped crying for a moment and examined the ring. It was the same one she had given her husband when they had married nearly sixty years before. She placed the ring on her own finger and began to weep anew, certain now that her husband had been swallowed by the dolphin.

"Do not cry, old woman," said the dolphin. "Your husband gave this ring to me and sent me to find you. He is waiting for you in his kingdom beneath the sea. Climb now onto my back and I will take you to him."

The fisherman's wife stared again into the dolphin's eyes and stopped crying. "I see that you are not a terrible shark, as I at first feared," she finally said. "And I would willingly go anywhere to see my beloved husband once more."

And she stood up in the boat, surprised to find her body supple. She moved smoothly and easily and without the pain in her bones she had been accustomed to for years. "What is this!" she cried out in awe. "My body feels young again! I feel as strong as when I was a girl."

"Look into my eyes once more," said the dolphin, "and I will be your mirror."

And the woman looked into the dolphin's eyes which were like silver glass and saw a lovely young face staring back at her. She began to laugh with Joy.

"Your husband's ring which you placed on your finger," began the dolphin, "has returned you to love's beginning, to the age at which you first married. Climb now upon my back, for I am your maid of honor and have come to lead you to your second and final wedding."

The fisherman's wife-to-be climbed easily onto the dolphin's back, wrapped in her beautiful silver and gold robe, which now seemed to her to be a wedding dress and not a shroud. Her fear was erased and did not return even when the water closed over her eyes. In a trance she watched the ocean world coming to life around her. She breathed deeply and inhaled the salty cold water into her lungs, and it felt very good to do so. Each breath of cold, salty water seemed to wake her up, until at last she felt she would burst if she were to be any more awake.

The Joyfish

At the same time, in the underwater cavern, the Joyfish swam to and fro in a frenzy of excitement, making preparations for the wedding.

"It is almost time for that which I was promised many millennia ago," the Joyfish cried out, swimming in wild circles in the cavern. "It is almost time for me to be truly born. Long, long have I awaited this day!"

At last all was ready. The man who used to be a fisherman and the woman who used to be a fisherman's wife stood side by side on the ocean floor. The Joyfish hovered in the water before them.

"In the name of the Father and the Mother," the Joyfish spoke.

"In the name of Love."

"In the name of Joy."

The two lovers waited to be joined.

The Joyfish rubbed a scale from his side. It fell to the ocean floor where it at once took root and grew into a miraculous plant with tendrils of silver and gold winding into the ocean for miles in all directions.

"I now pronounce you Husband and Wife," said the Joyfish. And as the two lovers kissed, the Joyfish called, "Let it be done!"

As if in response to his words, the ocean waters grew wild, and there raged a great storm beneath the sea. The husband and wife clung tightly to each other and to the tendrils of the miraculous sea plant, which wrapped around their arm and legs, holding them safe against the storm. The Joyfish swam between and around their bodies with silver and gold threads in his mouth. The frenzy and passion of the storm lasted for many months, during which time the husband and wife came to know and love each other very well, bound together as they were by the tendrils of the sea plant and by the silver and gold threads of the Joyfish.

One day, at last, all went calm. The husband and wife, as though waking from a dream, found themselves once again in the upper world, sailing in a small boat that had once belonged to an old fisherman. A fierce rainbow burned above them and cast strange colors upon their shimmering robes. They stared into the rainbow and then into each other's eyes and smiled. Suddenly, they heard a tiny cry. Lying at their feet was the most beautiful baby they had ever seen. Its eyes were liquid golden orbs, and its skin seemed to contain all the colors of the rainbow and to shine with an inner light. Wrapped snugly around the baby was a blanket woven of silver and gold threads. The baby smiled and reached out its tiny arms to be held. The husband and wife knelt before the baby and bowed their heads, then gathered it up in their arms. "Let us call the baby Joy," said the father.

Though the sea was perfectly still, the boat moved of its own accord and carried the new family away from the rainbow to the other edge of the sea, where another world was waiting for them, a world such as has been promised to all of us when we are only ready to receive it.

Acknowledgements

I could never have finished this book without the help of my family and friends. I am forever indebted to Sarah McBride and Teresa Nimry, my beloved sisters, who have always encouraged and supported my creative ventures.

I am also deeply—and alphabetically—grateful to:

Billie Anderson, whose quick wit and refined sensibilities enrich my life;

Nancy Scott Hanway and Karen Holman, Gemini sisters and writing partners of the highest order;

Lynn Keating, whose empathic gifts soothe me and lift my spirits;

Teri Kruse-Bauer, who has been listening to my tales since we were twelve years old;

Alice Maupin, bird-singer extraordinaire, who never holds my imperfections against me;

Greg Michaelson, my friend of many lifetimes, whose enthusiasm for my music and writing sustains me;

Sheila O'Connor and Tim Frederick, in whose attic I finished writing a chapter, and whose interest in this tale encouraged me;

Stevie Pannell, a thoughtful and compassionate listener masquerading as an imp;

Colleen Passard, whose wise counsel and keen insights inform my thinking;

Robert Sigovich, a.k.a. Ziggy, a true friend I've never seen, who helped me at the most crucial juncture—the last and longest mile—sending encouragement and comments, chapter by chapter.

Larry Steelman, whose careful attention amazes me.

Thank you also to:

Alexandra Balasa, Raluca Balasa, Joan Busch, Astrid Chaidez, Otis Clarke, Anna Garwood, Reed Hill, Tammy Huang-Anacleto, Tom Izzo,

Acknowledgements

Joanne Kennedy, Kimberly Kim, Tracy Klein, Ann Kong, Huggy Bear McBride, Ian McBride, Stephanie McBride, Kathy Myers, Nadir Nimry, Ziad Nimry, Shannon Couture O'Flinn, Ernie Petito, Josie Rawson, Laura Rawson, Mark Rawson, Aubrie Schmidt, Jennifer Son, and Kristin Turk, who have supported me in so many ways over the phone, via zoom, or in person;

John W. Hedenberg, Robert Mezey, Bill Pierce, James Semans, and Chuck Shockley, all departed now;

Alan Dino Hebel and Ian Koviak of theBook-Designers for their inspiring cover and interior design;

Sergio Angulo, my spiritual son, for his enthusiastic encouragement and financial support during the creation of this book;

And last, but never least, Eric Rawson, my husband, best friend, soulmate, and companion on my journey through this world.